I Believe In You

Barbara Conklin

BANTAM BOOKS
TORONTO • NEW YORK • LONDON • SYDNEY • AUCKLAND

RL 6, IL age 11 and up

I BELIEVE IN YOU
A Bantam Book / September 1984
Reprinted 1985

Sweet Dreams and its associated logo are registered trademarks of Bantam Books, Inc. Registered in U.S. Patent and Trademark Office and elsewhere.

Cover photo by Pat Hill

All rights reserved.
Copyright © 1984 by Barbara Conklin and Cloverdale Press Inc.
This book may not be reproduced in whole or in part, by mimeograph or any other means, without permission.
For information address: Bantam Books, Inc.

ISBN 0-553-24180-X

Published simultaneously in the United States and Canada

Bantam Books are published by Bantam Books, Inc. Its trademark, consisting of the words "Bantam Books" and the portrayal of a rooster, is registered in U.S. Patent and Trademark Office and in other countries. Marca Registrada. Bantam Books, Inc., 666 Fifth Avenue, New York, New York 10103.

Printed and bound in Great Britain by Hunt Barnard Printing Ltd.

O 0 9 8 7 6 5 4 3 2 1

There is a city in the great state of Oregon called Newport. It snuggles up cozily to the Pacific Ocean in the Pacific Northwest, and it is celebrating one hundred years of existence. This dedication is to the people of Newport, specifically Pat and Jean Melton who lured us to the area, to the students and faculty of Lincoln Junior High and Newport High School, to KNPT, their fine radio station, to Natalie Barnes of the Newport Times *and Sgt. Rothaermel of the Newport Police Department. A special thanks to the Snow girls of Princeton, Illinois. Amy, Lisa, and Susie Snow, may you always have sweet dreams.*

I Believe In You

Chapter One

It was a beautiful June afternoon, a few days into summer vacation, and I should have been ecstatic. I had every reason to be happy. I'd finished my junior year and was finally a senior, and I was going to my favorite place in the whole world the next day! But I wasn't ecstatic. And I wasn't fooling my best friend, Jessica, into thinking I was, either.

"Penny, I thought you adored your summers in Oregon," she said, flopping onto my bed and stretching her long, slim legs in front of her. "Last year you were upset because you couldn't go, and this year you're not even excited." She pushed her dark hair out of her eyes. "You'll be seeing your friends Giddy and Jan again. And you know what great times you three have together."

I tucked a few tank tops into my suitcase, which lay open on the floor. "Yeah, we used to run all over Newport together," I said sighing.

"I guess I'm just a bit nervous. Oh, Jessica, so much has happened since the last time I saw them!"

"Sure has. You're a senior now, older, more mature. Just look at you. Two years ago you were a skinny, little fourteen-year-old with glasses and frizzy brown hair. Now you've got a great figure; your contact lenses show off those gorgeous hazel eyes; and your new haircut gives you fantastic, shiny waves." I gave Jessica a dirty look. She laughed. "Oh, don't get me wrong, you were cute back then. But you're a knockout now. Anyway, there's nothing to be nervous about."

I didn't say a word, just sat on the floor and continued putting clothes into my suitcase.

"Personally I'd give anything to be going to Newport with you. There's not much to do in Carousel, Ohio, during the summer. Dan's going to Virginia; so I won't have a boyfriend. You'll be in Oregon; so I won't have a best friend. The only person who'll be around is Rommie, and her parents have gotten overprotective since your moped accident. They never let her do anything fun, and she can't go anywhere unless they drive her."

Jessica had pushed the right button—my

panic button. I felt like my whole chest was caving in. That dumb, crummy accident on Rommie's moped that no operation could fix. I blinked back my tears and bit my lower lip.

"Please, let's not talk about that," I told Jessica firmly.

"I'm sorry, Penny, that was really insensitive of me. I'm really sorry."

I got up and went to my white-painted chest of drawers, which I'd decorated the summer before with Pennsylvania Dutch decals. On the top of the chest a long line of trophies stood gleaming. Swimming trophies, tennis trophies, and more swimming trophies. I glanced over at my favorite one, first place in the state championship for the butterfly stroke. I looked away quickly.

"It *will* be wonderful to see Giddy and Jan again," I admitted to Jessica. "We were a great threesome, and great swimmers. And when we formed our relay team, no one could beat us. Giddy had a perfect crawl, Jan had the fastest breaststroke I've ever seen—"

"And we all know about your butterfly," Jessica interrupted.

"What a great team we made. All we did that summer was swim. We'd do laps and sprints, work on our form, time one another, push our speeds. On the days it'd be pouring, we'd work out in the indoor pool. And winning! It was even better sharing first place with my friends than winning by myself at school meets. We worked together in a really special way. It was the best summer."

"You never told me," Jessica said, "how they took the news of your accident. I bet they were amazed to hear you're not swimming anymore.

I let my breath out in a rush and faced my friend squarely. "I never told them," I said steadily. "I just never told them." Abandoning my packing, I sank onto the bed next to Jessica. "They think I'm still the expert swimmer they had so much fun with at the Newport municipal pool two years ago. They think I'm still terrific on the tennis court. I never told them about my accident, about my hip that doesn't work the way it should, even after two operations. I just don't want to face them. I'd rather not go at all."

Jessica looked at me in disbelief and finally said in a low, soft voice, "They'll understand. I know you really miss your sports, but there'll be other fun things to do. And, Penny, this will be your last summer in Newport before your grandfather sells his house."

I stared at my hands, suddenly intent on my nails, so that Jessica wouldn't see the tears that were forming in my eyes. "Yeah," I said. "Then Grandad will go live in some old rest home."

"Why doesn't he just come back to Ohio with you?" Jessica asked. She pushed her long, silky hair out of her face.

"No way!" I told her. "Grandad would never leave Oregon, you know that! He was born there, and he raised my mother there."

We both sat in silence again after my outburst. I'm explosive on the subject of my grandfather because I love him so much and can't bear to see him grow old.

Slowly Jessica looked at me and continued our previous conversation. "I can't get over your not telling Giddy and Jan about the accident," she said hesitantly. "But don't worry; if they're the kind of friends you say they are, it will be OK. You'll see."

I held my breath for a second as I watched her encouraging smile grow. And then I was smiling with her. I nodded my head. "You're right. It *will* be OK. Giddy and Jan *will* understand."

But I was still upset. It wasn't Giddy and Jan—I knew Jessica was right, my injury wouldn't matter to them, and we'd still be friends. But what I wanted more than anything was to be able to swim and play other sports. It had been a year since the accident, a year since I'd had a good hard swim or tennis game. But I could still imagine the physical sensations of those sports. And I knew I'd never have them again—never.

Chapter Two

As I looked at my father standing at the stove, I suddenly realized how much I was going to miss him. Dad was looking more like a gym teacher than what he really was, an English teacher for the eighth grade at Carousel Junior High. Since school had ended, he let his dark, curly hair grow a little longer than usual, and he had started wearing the faded T-shirts and old, white sailing pants that were his summer uniform.

He wasn't coming to Newport with my mother, brother, and me because of a book he was going to write. He'd landed a good contract for a novel, and with the rest of us gone, he'd have the peace and quiet he needed to write. Don't get me wrong. We weren't going off on a vacation and leaving poor Dad at home to work. We were going to be working awfully hard, too. We were going to Newport to help my grandfather close up his house. Mom said it would be pretty easy for him to find a buyer. So we'd be putting a small amount of his furniture in storage, selling most of it, sorting through everything, cleaning up, and maybe even doing some minor repairs.

"I picked up your plane tickets today," Dad told Mom. "We were lucky that there was that deal this summer for kids under twelve to fly free with an adult."

I fantasized about my eight-year-old brother getting on the wrong plane with some other people and flying off in the opposite direction. What a relief that would be. Frankie could be a real pain some of the time—most of the time. He had the biggest mouth, and once he got hold of a secret, it wasn't secret too long.

"Um-mm," my father murmured, tasting the hot potato-and-sausage soup before he carried it to the table.

I stared over at Frankie. "Did you wash your hands?" I asked him.

He made a face at me but got up and washed them in the kitchen sink. He knew if he didn't, he'd be hearing from Mom soon enough. I'd really only said it to bother him, but I was sorry when I heard my mother sigh loudly. I knew she was tired of packing and listening to Frankie and me bicker.

Mom looked gorgeous for a woman of forty-two. She has a beautiful figure because she's in great shape, always stretching and stuff. Her eyes are blue most of the time, but that day they looked blue-gray. She wore her copper-colored hair brushed free and long so that it swirled around her shoulders.

"Kids, remember to pack your rain gear," she said tiredly. "You know how it can storm in Oregon, even in the summer."

"Penny," Dad said, watching me with concern, "you don't look too excited. What's bothering you?"

My mother looked up, the ladle suspended in midair as she stopped dishing soup. She'd been too busy to notice I wasn't exactly brimming over with joy. She glanced at me and then at my father. "I think she feels the same way I do, Andrew," she told my father. "This will be our first trip to Newport without you. It seems so strange."

"That's right," I said. *Our first trip to Newport when I can't swim or play tennis,* I thought.

Mom remembered the biscuits, got up, and brought the basket to the table. Frankie grabbed at one, and the whole basket slid out of Mom's hand and right into his lap. I tried to help him put the biscuits back, but he pulled away from me. "I can do it myself!" he hissed.

My mother put her hand up to her head. "Please, kids, no arguing. I'm getting a headache."

My mother teaches home ec at Carousel High and is used to kids arguing, but she always claims she can't stand it from Frankie and me.

My father frowned at both of us. Then, to move the conversation on to a more pleasant topic, he said, "I guess you'll be looking forward to lots of swimming and sunning, Penny."

Choking on my soup, I reached for some iced tea.

"Swimming?" Frankie said. "Penny's too chicken to swim now." An entire biscuit disappeared into his mouth.

"Don't talk with your mouth full," my father said.

"And don't say such mean things about your sister," my mother added. "Penny will get back to her sports when she feels strong enough." She smiled gently at me. "But, honey, you know the doctor said you should be getting some exercise. She said it would help your hip to heal."

"That's what I mean. She's chicken!" Frankie shouted triumphantly.

I gave my brother a dirty look.

"Oh, stop it," Mom said to him.

Then she turned to me. "Don't worry about it. You're sensible. You'll do what's best for your hip, I know. Now, you," she said to my father, "have got to promise me that you'll finish your book. You'll certainly have all the quiet you ever dreamed of." I was glad she'd changed the subject before we got into another discussion about the accident. Things were bad enough without having to talk about that.

"Oh, I'll finish," Dad said. "It should be fairly easy now that the first two drafts are done. It's just a matter of fine tuning at this point. With a whole summer of quiet and my new typewriter, I'll finish for sure."

"And just let the garden go. Don't give in and let it run you," my mother told him. "I don't want you out there weeding when you should be writing."

"But I do my best thinking when I'm weeding," Dad argued.

"But you said most of the thinking is

over," she came back. Dad would let her have the last word. He always did. He finished his soup quietly.

It seemed like the whole family was arguing. I guess I wasn't the only one who was worried about the summer. Dad had the book to finish, Mom had Grandad's house to get in order, and they both were probably nervous about being apart for three months. And Frankie, well—Frankie always liked to pester me.

I thought of our last summer in Newport. Giddy, Jan, and I had entered every race the Newport pool sponsored and won all of them. It had been the best time of my life. But that was before the accident. Things were different now.

I guess my family had visited Newport, Oregon, every summer since I was born, and it had always been wonderful, climbing the rugged cliffs that ran along the Pacific Ocean, picking up agates, and watching the boats slide down past the horizon. On the Fourth of July, the whole family would take off to go fishing or hiking into the pines. Afterward we'd watch the most amazing fireworks over the bay.

We hadn't gone the last summer because

of my accident and because my parents had decided to teach summer school. Giddy, Jan, and I had written long letters. They had told me about every swim meet at the pool. I caught myself starting to sigh out loud.

"Come on, Penny," my father said, laughing, "it won't be that bad. I'm sure you can get in the pool and paddle around, at least."

But I knew I wouldn't even want to go to the pool. And no matter how I tried, I couldn't get the picture of the three of us winning meet after meet out of my mind. What was I going to do all summer?

Chapter Three

Jessica has always been a nut! Maybe that's why I like her so much. She said a serious, final goodbye to me the next day at my kitchen door, and she placed a huge box of black and red licorice sticks in my hands. Then she handed me another box.

"Don't open it till you get to the airport," she cautioned me. "Swear!"

"I swear," I promised, and we hugged each other goodbye.

All the way to the airport I restrained myself from pushing and shoving and shaking the box until, finally, as my father slid into a parking space, I felt that we were close enough, and I ripped off the pink foil and yarn tie.

There, inside the shoe box, was one running shoe. Tiger Lady X-Caliber, the box said. Jessica and I had seen the shoes in Goodman's Sport Center just a week before, and I had commented on how much I liked the gray and maroon combination. Jessica had liked the gray with navy. Now I held one shoe, gray with maroon trim. A beautiful running shoe—but *one* shoe?

"It's the left one," Frankie said, looking over my shoulder.

"So what?"

"What is it?" Mom asked.

"Jessica gave me a present besides the licorice—one running show. I guess something happened, and she just forgot to put in the other shoe," I said, admiring the one I had. *She's telling me to run*, I thought, *but she knows I can't.*

I placed the lonely shoe back in the soft white tissue paper that lined the box. *Jessica shouldn't have spent all that money*, I thought, *especially since I won't use them. Even if I did have both.*

Just fifteen minutes before the plane was due to take off, I saw Jessica standing in a crowd of people, waving the other running shoe in the air.

"Penny!" she yelled. "It was the only way I could talk my mom into driving me over. I told her I'd forgotten to give you the other half of your present!"

Mrs. Carrington would forgive her later, I was sure. We hugged goodbye again, and before I knew it, it was time to board. Jessica whispered in my ear at the very last minute. "It's going to be OK, Penny. I just know it. The next time you see me, you'll be telling me that you just had the best summer ever!"

"Thanks," I told her. I didn't bother to mention that I couldn't use her present. I didn't want to hurt her feelings. And she'd come all the way to the airport just to give me that one last bit of assurance. She's the kind of friend everyone ought to have.

It seemed so strange to be boarding the plane without my father. He had a misty look in his eyes when I finally gave him a hug and kiss goodbye. My mother looked like she was holding back a tear or two herself.

We had to change planes in Chicago; so we weren't on that first one very long. It was the only connection my father could make to take us from Carousel, Ohio, into Eugene, Oregon. Then, in Eugene my grandfather would meet us and drive us into Newport, about two hours away.

In Chicago my mother arranged our seats so that both Frankie and I could have a window. The seats were in rows of three, and

Frankie and my mother sat across the aisle from me with a man on the aisle seat. A woman and her mother shared my section of three seats. The old lady had a terrible hacking cough, and I kept turning my face toward the window so that I wouldn't catch whatever it was she had.

She smiled a couple of times at me and called me honey when she asked me what part of Oregon I was traveling to. Shortly after the seat belt sign went off, she fell asleep and started to snore, to the obvious embarrassment of her daughter, who kept nudging her whenever the snoring got too loud.

Floating peacefully above the clouds, I began thinking about Giddy and Jan. I pictured Giddy, tall and thin, pushing her dark hair out of her dark brown eyes, and tiny Jan with her kinky blond curls and pale white skin. I wondered how they'd have changed in two years. I was sure they'd look a little different, but they'd be the same in the important ways. Not like me. I studied my leg thoughtfully. I had no scars from the accident; so you couldn't tell by looking at me that there had been so much damage to my right side.

My right hip began to get stiff and painful like it did when I sat too long in the movies, and I started to rub the top of my leg. My mother bent over the man's newspaper and motioned to me. "Penny, why don't you take a short walk and stretch it a bit."

I shook my head energetically and turned away, embarrassed. Now the man sitting beside my mother knew there was something wrong with me. Parents can be so frustrating at times.

I guess I was really exhausted from all that packing because I dozed off into a heavy sleep. Before I knew it, the flight attendant woke me and asked me to raise the back of my seat. The loudspeaker system came alive. "We will be landing at Mahlon Sweet Field, Eugene, Oregon, in eight minutes," the pilot's voice announced. "We hope you have enjoyed your flight with us. Please fasten your seat belts and prepare for landing."

Newport, here I come, I thought, and I didn't know whether to be excited or scared stiff.

Chapter Four

I felt that I could smell the velvety pines even before I stepped out of the plane. The air was clean and crisp, and because we had traveled three hours back in time, it was still afternoon, not much later than when we had left.

The airport building was gray and pink. I kept an eye out for my grandfather as we picked up our luggage. Usually he would have been waiting when our plane landed, but that day his shock of white hair wasn't to be seen anywhere in the crowd. After a few minutes we drifted out to the parking lot.

"Look for a monster of a blue Buick," Mom told Frankie, who didn't remember too much about Grandad or his old car. On our last trip Frankie had been only six.

Finally, after peering over the cars streaming into the lot, we decided to sit down on the plastic seats that lined one side of the building. Yellow, blue, red. We each had our own color.

I looked at the mountains surrounding us. They were as beautiful as I had remembered them, and I was glad to be back. I loved those tall pines. They grew so thick that you could barely pass between them and so tall you had to tilt your head back as far as you could to see the tops. *They'll never have to worry about Christmas trees here,* I thought.

My mother pulled us both to our feet. "Come on, let's take your picture and send it home to your father." She walked over to a stone wall, right under the airport sign, and snapped a Polaroid picture of Frankie and me. Frankie was making a stupid face, as usual, and just when the camera clicked, I blinked.

I walked away from the wall, and Frankie sat down on the curb. I heard my mother moan when she looked at the developing picture. First it was a tannish color, and then, as I watched, the details slowly started to appear. It was awful, and I moaned, too.

"Oh my," Mom said, frowning. "You have your eyes closed again, Penny. How do you always manage that? Let me take another one."

Frankie and I stood in front of the sign.

This time, Frankie smiled his crooked grin, and I forced myself not to blink. It was hard to do because the sun was glaring right in my eyes.

I watched as the second picture developed. It was bad, but not so awful as the first one. Mom smiled and tucked it into her bag. "Good," she said. "Now let's look around and try to find Grandad. It's strange that he's late."

That's when I saw the old Buick turning into the parking lot. My grandfather was on the passenger side, waving at us like crazy as the car pulled up to the curb.

The driver was just about my age. Tall and thin, he had to unfold his long legs from behind the steering wheel before he could swing them out the open door. I watched him walk around the car and reach in to help my grandfather struggle out.

Grandad looked much older. His hair seemed even whiter than before, and more scalp was showing through it. He didn't seem quite so tall as he had, or was he just stooped over more? There were a lot of wrinkles on his forehead and under his eyes, and he was thinner than ever. Maybe too thin.

He hugged and kissed us all. It was so

great to see him again. My mother had tears streaming down her cheeks, and I had to swallow hard to keep mine back. I hate to cry in public. Frankie just stood there, not really knowing what to do.

"I just can't believe it," my grandfather said as he took one step backward to look at my little brother. He reached down to give Frankie a bear hug, but changing his mind, he thrust out a huge hand toward Frankie's small one. It made Frankie break into a silly grin, and I could tell that they were going to get along just fine.

All the time this was going on, I had the uncanny feeling that my grandfather's driver was looking me over—carefully. I could feel his eyes riveted on me, and after a few seconds, his gaze seemed to force me to look at him. What a weird feeling!

I always notice eyes first. They seem to tell the most about a person. I have a teacher back in Carousel who is as cold as her ice-blue eyes. They seem to cut you dead when you have to tell her that your homework is late. And then there's Ms. Evans, who has warm, brown eyes. If your homework is late, she tries to find out why you didn't have enough time to finish, and then she makes suggestions for using your time more wisely, but she does it all in a caring, considerate way. It's kind of funny, but after that, you really knock yourself out to finish every assignment for her.

Oh, yes, eyes do give people away, and this guy standing in front of me, studying me, had eyes the kind of dark blue that you see in deep lakes. He had to be a serious person.

He gave me the slightest hint of a smile, and I managed one back. My grandfather broke the spell. "Oh, I'm sorry. This is Bill Davis. He's been helping me around the house and doing chores for me. Dr. Dunn just won't let me drive myself around anymore."

After the introductions, Bill and Frankie stashed our luggage in the trunk. I watched Bill resettle my grandfather in the passenger seat before climbing behind the wheel. Frankie, my mom, and I got in the back.

"Do you still have Rusty?" Frankie piped up as we pulled away from the curb.

Grandfather turned to look at Frankie and smiled. "Sure do. He's around and doing pretty well for his old age."

"Does he still wait by your chair and beg for scraps?" Frankie asked.

"He still does," my grandfather said, laughing. "That dog doesn't change much, except to get old like me. He just sits there and waits for me to hand him a bit of toast or a piece of pork chop. And he loves french fries."

"Dad, don't tell me you eat pork chops and french fries. They are definitely not on your diet!" My grandfather coughed and mumbled something. My mother just sat back and sighed. "You probably still gorge yourself with ice cream, too." I wished Frankie hadn't brought up the subject at all.

I settled myself in the corner of the big car and closed my eyes for a moment. I wondered what Giddy and Jan were doing right then. Maybe they'd be at the pool. When I opened my eyes again, I had the sensation of our sailing along, forests on both sides. Frankie's attention was caught by a deer grazing peacefully in a distant meadow, and my mother exclaimed over the beauty of it all.

My grandfather began to talk about his house and how much he hated to leave it, but his doctor had advised it. Then suddenly he twisted in his seat and looked back at me. "And how's my girl doing?" he asked, smiling warmly at me. "How's the leg? Your mother says you're fine now." I saw Bill's hand go up and adjust the rearview mirror. He was looking at me again!

"I'm OK," I said coldly.

"She's doing just fine," my mother added, giving me one of her funny looks that says, "Be nice." I absolutely hated it whenever anyone asked me how my leg was. Why didn't they forget it? Just having them ask about my leg made it hurt, and now I felt a cramp in the back of my knee. All I wanted to do was get to Newport and stretch a little.

The rest of the ride went smoothly. My mother and grandfather talked over old times, Frankie fell asleep against Mom's shoulder, and Bill kept adjusting that dumb mirror until I thought I would scream.

I figured two could play his staring game; so I studied his back. His shoulders were narrow, but they looked strong. His hair was a very rich, dark brown, with a tiny hint of red. Once in a while he would push a few strands away from his eyes. His hair wasn't parted on any particular side; it was kind of tousled. Not sloppily tousled, but kind of comfortable, if you know what I mean. I could see his profile when he checked on the traffic at intersections. His nose was straight, and his mouth seemed soft and kind.

Finally we got to Newport. Frankie was awake now, and my mother was saying how happy she was to be back in her old hometown at last. She always gets very sentimental as we ride into Newport for the first time.

"I've got a roast beef I made last night," my grandfather announced as Bill drove the car down to the beach road. "We can have sandwiches and some of my world-renowned potato salad. And I made your favorite cake, Louise."

"But you're not supposed to be in that kitchen at all," my mother said. "Dad, you're going against all the doctor's orders!"

My grandfather laughed. "If I couldn't cook a little once in a while, I'd surely dry up and die!" he exclaimed. "That's what's worrying me about going off to that old people's home. I don't think they're going to let me poke around in their kitchen."

My mother touched his shoulder, scooting forward so that she could be closer to him. "It's not called an old people's home, Dad. It's a home for retired people. And I've told you over and over again that you should come back to Carousel with us. Now that the time has finally come for you to sell the old place, it wouldn't be so bad with us."

My grandfather threw back his head and laughed. "Louise, I was born in Newport and grew up in my father's general store. I went to school in Newport, married, and raised you here. This is where I intend to stay. Why should I spoil it all now?"

The car pulled around a curve, and there was Grandad's house, just as I remembered it. It sits on the edge of a cliff above the beach. When I was little, I used to think it was going to topple right into the ocean with the next big storm. It's large and majestic, with huge windows in every room. On sunny days light streams in, making everything glow. On rainy days, it's cozy because the storm literally rages all around while you're snuggled up dry inside.

That day was sunny and the ocean sparkled down below as we pulled up to the house. Everything was the same. I wanted to change into a bathing suit, run down the rickety old steps to the beach, and have a long, hard swim. Of course, with my leg I couldn't do that. The thought hurt for a moment, but I was too happy to mope that day. My heart fluttered, and I drew in my breath with excitement. We were really there at last.

Chapter Five

As soon as Bill pulled the car to a stop by the back door, I jumped out and took a deep breath, filling my lungs with ocean air. I dashed in the back door and into the kitchen. The promised carrot cake stood on a rack on the counter.

I ran through the stately, living room, filled with highly polished furniture to the sun porch, which runs across the whole front of the house. It's my favorite place in the house. Tiny panes of glass enclose the porch that looks right down onto the beach. It's a great place to watch the sunset on a cold night, and it's the best place to watch a storm roll in over the ocean.

Beyond the sun porch is a small wooden patio, beaten into a weathered gray color by years of sun and wind. I stepped outside and just stared at the water and sky. The sea gulls, which had gathered on a cluster of rocks, cried out, then fluttered their wings and flew off as though they had just dropped by to welcome me. I waved at them and even called out a hello. I was so glad to be in Newport at last! Then I heard my mother yell for me, and I made my way back into the kitchen, where Bill had just dumped our luggage.

"Where do you want these?" he asked, his first whole sentence since we'd met. In the two-hour trip from Eugene, he hadn't spoken a word.

"I've taken to sleeping in one of the downstairs bedrooms. It's easier on me," my grandfather told my mother. "So you three can take upstairs bedrooms, I thought maybe the front ones. Then you can all have a view of the ocean."

Bill began to drag the luggage upstairs. I grabbed my own bags and followed him up. "Which ones go where?" he asked me in the upstairs hallway.

My mother spoke up right behind us. "I'll take the pink room," she said. "That way Frankie can have the adjoining room. Penny, you take my old bedroom. It's big but cozy, and it's got the nicest view of the ocean. You've always loved the wallpaper in there. And this summer I want you to have the best!"

I dragged my bags into the end room, and I began to study that special wallpaper. It was a repeating series of drawings of two girls, a little older in each successive picture. The first showed them playing on the sand with their shovels and buckets. In the second picture the lighter-haired one was on a swing entwined with tiny flowers while the darker girl pushed her, laughing. The third picture showed them sitting together on an old porch reading, a stack of books piled at their feet. In the next drawing two boys walked beside them. And in the final drawing, the girls waved goodbye to each other. Each one was holding onto a boy's hand. I looked again at the last drawing. The girls seemed to be happy, but as I examined it more closely, I could see that the artist wanted you to know that they were sad, too. Laced around each picture were tiny violets. I touched a leaf gently and could almost feel the softness of the real leaf.

That room had always been my mother's, but now she was letting me have it. I knew she wanted me to be especially happy because she felt bad that I'd missed the summer before. And maybe, also, to make up a little for the accident.

My mother appeared in the doorway.

"How about something to eat before we unpack?" she asked me. "As usual, your grandfather fussed over a meal for us. Now that I'm here, I'm going to make sure he doesn't do it again."

I followed her down the long hall. "But why do you worry about him? He's so skinny, he can't be eating much."

"You know as well as I do that it's not how thin or how fat you are. After a heart attack, you have to eat certain foods to keep your veins clear and your heart muscle strong. Some foods work against you."

I should have known. Last year I'd written a paper on just that subject, but somehow I'd never applied what I'd learned to my own grandfather. He loved food so much, and he adored cooking.

Frankie was already down in the dining room when we reached it, and I heard Grandad asking Bill to stay and eat with us.

"I can't, but thanks, anyway," he said politely. "My grandmother wants me to buy some fish for dinner; so I'd better get going." He walked toward the kitchen, and I remembered I'd seen an old, beat-up Volkswagen Bug in the driveway when we'd pulled up. It had been hidden under the trees, but I could just see the faded yellow car.

I heard him start it, and I turned to my grandfather, saying "I've never seen him before."

"Oh, yes, you have," he told me, going to the refrigerator to get the dinner he'd prepared. My mother was right behind him.

"You sit down, Dad," she said to him. "From now on, I'm in charge of this kitchen!"

My grandfather gave up easily this time. "OK, I'll just start up the coffeepot," he said, smiling, and I knew he was really happy to have us all back in the old house again.

He filled the aluminum pot with cold water, measured in the coffee for the basket, and then plugged it in. Weary, he sat down on the nearest kitchen chair.

I dropped down on one next to him, suddenly feeling very tired myself, jet lag, I supposed. It was three hours later back home, after all. "No, I don't remember Bill," I insisted.

"He's really changed a lot," Grandad said. "Do you remember the kid who used to cut my grass and sometimes pull out the flowers instead of the weeds when you were here last?"

"Sure," I told him, "a fat kid. But not Bill Davis. That guy was kind of roly-poly with pimples on his face."

"That's him," my grandfather said, a twinkle in his eyes.

"It couldn't be the same guy," I told my Grandad. "Bill is tall and skinny, and he has a nice complexion. He's really pretty good-looking."

"Ah-ha, you've noticed!" my grandfather said, and his laughter filled the kitchen. "I thought you were kind of quiet in the backseat all that time. Bill *has* changed a lot. He's a California kid, born and raised there. The summer you were here, he was just visiting his grandparents and making a little extra money doing some work on my yard. As it turned out, Bill never got to go back home to California. His folks were killed in a plane crash. So Bill's summer never ended. He could never go back. There was nothing to go back to." I felt a sudden compassion for Bill. It must have been a nightmare for him. Grandad continued. "He lives with his grandparents now, and he's a devoted grandson from everything I hear. And every night, just before the sun goes down, you can see him running along the beach here. He's like a streak of lightning. You have to look fast, or you'll miss him," he joked.

I better understood those dark blue eyes now. It wasn't just the color, it was something else, a seriousness and a sensitivity that I hadn't seen in any other boy's eyes before.

I thought about that for a while, then put Bill out of my mind and asked my grandfather if he'd seen Giddy and Jan lately.

"They dropped by a couple months ago, brought me some pickled beets from Giddy's mother," he said, smiling at me. "I told them way back then that you might make it here this summer, and they acted real happy at the thought. Why don't you give them a call?"

"Tomorrow," my mother said, slicing the roast beef. "We've had a big day, and we have all that unpacking to do."

"I don't think you'll be seeing much of them, unless you plan to live at the pool," Grandad said. "They both applied for jobs as lifeguards. I ran into Giddy's mother in the market a few weeks back, and she said they both passed the tests and will be full-time guards all summer long."

Giddy and Jan lifeguards! Wow! I could remember years ago when we sat on the bleachers inside the pool area and talked about how fantastic that job would be! You'd be doing something you loved and getting paid for it. That had to be the best thing in the world. And there were some great-looking guys working at the pool, too.

"How lucky can you get!" I exclaimed to my grandfather. "Oh, now I can't wait to talk to them!"

"Tomorrow," my mother said again, and I knew she meant it.

Frankie had been shoveling his food into his mouth. "Can I have some more?" he asked. "I'm still hungry!"

"Oh, Frankie," my mother said and moaned theatrically. "You're going to make yourself sick eating so fast!"

"Not on my good food," my grandfather exclaimed. "Give him some more, Louise!"

"Dad, you'd better not spoil my children while we're here," she told him, trying not to smile. Suddenly she threw her arms around him, and he kissed her on the cheek. "It's so good to see you, Dad. It's been such a long, long time!"

I cleaned off the table while they were still talking about old times. After that, I walked out to the sun porch and just stood there looking through the glass. Then something down on the beach caught my eye. It was a boy running. I looked closer, then walked onto the patio, peering over the edge of the cliff. It was Bill Davis, running like a streak of lightning, just as Grandad had said he did at the end of each day. It looked as though his feet had wings, as though he were running above the ground. In minutes he was out of sight.

Chapter Six

Right after breakfast the next morning I called Giddy. I took one deep breath, and before I could exhale, Giddy was on the other end.

"Penny! I am so glad you're here again. I can't believe it's really you. Penny Snow!"

"The one and only!" I yelled back at her, laughing.

"Oh, Penny," she said, "it's been so long! I'm a lifeguard now. Jan is one, too! You have to come by the pool! I can't believe it's really you!"

It made me feel so good to hear my old friend so happy to hear from me that my laughter almost turned to tears. "I won't have much time for fun," I told her. "We're closing up the house for my grandfather. He's selling it, and we have to pack and sell everything."

There was a moment of silence on the other end, then Giddy said, "Tell you what.

Jan and I get off work at two this afternoon. We could come by and visit you—unless you want to come out to the pool. Hey, that's a great idea. Why don't you come by the pool and maybe do a few laps, and we'll talk a little."

"No, no, I won't have time," I said. "I'll be busy here, but by three I'm sure I'll have time for company. You two come over to the house."

"OK, Pen," Giddy agreed. "I know Jan's really excited about seeing you, too. So, we'll be there by three."

It was great just hearing Giddy's voice. I couldn't wait to see her and Jan. Giddy had to go to work; so we said goodbye until three.

"Penny," my mother said, coming into the room and sitting down on the couch, "I couldn't help overhearing and, well—I wanted to say that there's no reason you can't go to the pool. We have all summer to pack and get things settled here. You're not confined to the house. You should be out having fun."

"Oh, I just thought it would be nicer here," I told her, playing with the long phone cord. Somehow during the call I'd twisted it into an impossible knot.

She shook her head slowly from side to side. "Oh, Penny, don't do this to yourself.

This is your summer vacation. Don't let a little nervousness stop you from—"

A light tapping noise on the door interrupted my mother, and I was grateful. I didn't want another version of this lecture. I'd heard it before. Mom got up to get the door, and I could hear her greeting Bill. She had decided that we should start packing up the stuff in the garage first, and Grandad had called Bill to come over to help.

Well, I thought, *I got through that one OK. I'll be meeting Giddy and Jan in the house where I won't have to do anything except talk—and I can do that fine. No pools, no laps, no explanations.*

We spent most of the morning packing my grandfather's tools in the garage. He was sorry to see them go. At one point I thought I even noticed a tear in his eye.

Bill leaned over the box I was packing and whispered softly in my ear with an urgency I'd never heard before. "Don't you realize how miserable he is about leaving? How can you make him sell this house when he's so happy here?"

I looked up quickly, but Bill was already busy with something else. I didn't understand why he'd said that to me. Sure, we all knew

Grandad didn't want to go, but what could we do? He wouldn't come back to Ohio with us, and he definitely couldn't manage the house by himself anymore. I glanced at Bill, but he wouldn't look at me. Still, I could see he was upset. He really cared about my grandfather. Well, so did I, but there was no other choice. At least, I didn't think there was.

I put Bill's words out of my mind and continued wrapping tools and packing them in boxes. We worked hard all morning. Frankie wasn't really too much help, but then we hadn't brought him along for that reason. He spent most of his time with Rusty, which was great because we didn't have to worry about his being underfoot too much. He'd also found Bobby, a boy his age, who lived nearby.

At two-thirty Bill headed for home, and I went up to my room to get ready for my company. My mother disappeared into the kitchen to prepare a few snacks for my guests. Grandad decided it was time for his afternoon nap, and Frankie took off for Bobby's.

The sun porch looked inviting with the afternoon sun sparkling on the panes of glass. My grandfather had furnished it with white rattan chairs, all thickly padded with orange and white cushions. A swing hung from one end of the porch.

My mother had picked some flowers from my grandfather's garden, and she'd put them in a pretty vase on the glass-topped coffee table. She'd also put some chocolate-chip cookies and cheese crackers on a plate for us. A tall, frosty pitcher of lemonade and three glasses sat next to the plate.

I was fussing with my hair in the bathroom upstairs when I heard Giddy and Jan running up the beach stairs to the sun porch. I dashed down to meet my two old friends, and all at once we were laughing and talking, hugging and smiling. I saw my mother peeking out of the living room, and I grabbed her so that she could greet my guests, too. She stayed for only a few minutes, knowing that we wanted to be just the three of us, like old times. In the back of my head, though, I knew it could never be like old times, not really.

Jan's blue eyes sparkled as she jabbered merrily on about her new job at the pool. Her kinky, blond hair seemed even kinkier. She hadn't grown much since the last time I had seen her. She was still under five-two.

"Take one—take two." I offered Jan the

plate of cookies and laughed. "You're so tiny, you can afford the whole tray!"

Giddy smiled warmly at me. *The same old Giddy,* I thought happily, *except even prettier.* She had a deep tan, and her eyelashes were just touched with mascara, making her big brown eyes seem even bigger. She wore cut-off jeans and a white T-shirt with the name of the pool on it.

"We came right from work," she said proudly. "Penny, you have to come by and watch us. We have a class for kids in the morning. You'd really enjoy seeing it."

"If I get the time," I promised, knowing I would never go.

Giddy and I sprawled out on chairs, and Jan settled herself on the floor, leaning back against the porch wall. We talked about the pool, about Jan's new boyfriend who worked summers on one of the fishing boats, and about the guy Giddy was interested in, a lifeguard at the pool. Jan and Luke had been dating for two whole months, and it looked like Ron would be asking Giddy out any day now.

"If he doesn't, I'll just find something to ask him to!" Giddy told us, nibbling on a cheese cracker.

"Are you going out with anyone?" Jan asked, taking another swallow of her lemonade.

"Well, no one special." I got up and passed around the napkins.

"Let's go down to the beach," Giddy said as she grabbed two more crackers.

"Great," Jan said, taking another cookie.

Once we got down on the sand, we took off our shoes. The hot sand felt good between my toes. And it was great to be with my friends again. The three of us walked along the wet sand, dodging the curly waves of cold water dancing around our feet. We played in the surf, daring the waves to get us wet. Then we ran up to the dry sand and plopped down so we could talk and laugh and relax.

Suddenly, without warning, Giddy turned to me. She wasn't smiling, although her huge, brown eyes looked at me with warmth and caring. "We know all about your accident, Penny. There's no need to keep it from us. Your grandfather filled us in. But he said you were all better now. That's why I asked you to go swimming today."

"Oh!" I choked. It was all I could say for the moment. "But he's wrong. I mean, I'm better, but I still can't do things, you know, like swimming and all that. I could injure myself permanently. I guess my mother didn't tell him."

Jan looked miserable. "Penny, we didn't know."

"No," said Giddy. "We were told that you were fine now. You look fantastic and—"

"It's OK," I told them. "It's just that I have to be really careful. That's why I didn't come over to swim."

"I'm sorry, really sorry, Penny," Giddy said. "But listen, we could all go to the movies or go shopping down at the mall. We have a big, new one now. And there are a lot of other things we can do!"

"Oh, definitely," Jan said.

"Sure," I told them, feeling better about the whole thing.

"Listen, Penny, we've got to get back to the pool for a staff meeting," Giddy said. "But we'll call you and all get together soon."

"Great. It's been wonderful seeing you guys again."

"Likewise," Jan said, giving me a hug.

"Bye," Giddy called as they began trotting down the beach in the direction of town.

I walked back to the beach stairs very slowly. My feet felt heavy as I climbed them, and when I reached the porch, I sat down and just stared out at the ocean. The sun moved behind a gray cloud, and in minutes I could hear the splatter of rain on the sun porch windows. The downpour grew heavier, sounding as though glass beads were beating against the panes.

I remembered a rainstorm two summers before. It had been the first time Giddy, Jan, and I had competed together as a team, and the rain pounding against the pool had sounded the same way. I'd felt so close to my friends as we waited for our race to start.

I stared at my hands gloomily. *Now you're not part of anything, Penny Snow*, I told myself. *Now all you can do is sit around and listen to the rain.*

Chapter Seven

The boxes were really piling up. For four days I had worked with my mother and Bill, wrapping tools and gadgets, labeling boxes, taping them shut, and stacking them carefully in the corners of the huge garage. My grandfather sat on a high stool most of the time, directing the whole operation. Several times he pointed out tools he wanted to take with him to the rest home. And every time my mother reminded him that he would have absolutely no use for them there, it angered him.

"No cooking, no building anything," he muttered. "What the heck do they expect us to do at that old people's home?"

Sometimes I'd see Bill's lips tighten as if he, too, were angry that my grandfather had to go. But I didn't see any other choice. Grandad needed medical attention and relaxation. He sure couldn't get that in a big, old house. It was just too much work and too much worry for him to manage alone. I thought a lot about it but couldn't come up with an alternative. I knew Grandad would never leave Oregon and come back to Ohio with us.

To tell the truth, it annoyed me that Bill was sort of blaming us for my grandfather's unhappiness. We were all unhappy about the situation, too.

We finally talked about it one day after we had finished cleaning out the garage. I got us some iced tea, and we headed for the patio to catch the ocean breeze.

"Ugh," he groaned, lowering himself to the top step of the beach stairs. "That last load I carried was a back breaker."

He stood, did a little stretch, and then sat down again. He took a drink of his tea. That's when I asked him. "Bill, why are you so mad at us?"

"Mad?" he asked, surprised. "I'm not mad."

"Yes, you are. Every time Grandad gripes about going to the old folks' home, you look as if it's our fault."

"Oh, yeah," Bill said sheepishly. Then he looked directly in my eyes. "Well, it is in a way, isn't it?"

"Bill, we're only trying to do the best for him. He needs people around to look after him."

"It's just that he talks about the place as if there's nothing to do there. He's an active man. He'll be miserable sitting around all day long."

"I know," I told Bill. "I haven't seen the home. But I know there's a place back in Ohio where old people do most of the work themselves. They're very active, but they have help when they need it. I wish there were a place like that around here."

"Me, too." Bill said, sighing. "Penny, we've got to think of something."

"I know," I agreed. "I understand how awful it is to have to sit around when you're used to lots of activity."

"What do you mean?" Bill asked.

"Oh, well, since the accident I haven't been able to play all the sports I used to. It's really changed my life, and I don't like it."

"What accident?" Bill asked, turning to look at me. "Was that what your grandfather meant when he asked about your leg as we were driving from the airport?"

"Yes. Can't you tell? I walk funny."

"You don't walk funny." There was a

moment of silence. "Tell me about the accident," Bill finally said.

"I had a spill off the back of a moped, and my right leg and hip were injured. I've had two operations, but I'll never be the same. I used to be a great swimmer," I mused. "Back home I was the star of the swim team. I was on the tennis team, too, and I loved to ski. Then I had the accident. I can't do any of those sports now. I'll always be a little too slow to win any kind of competition."

"So, now you aren't into any sport—you don't do anything?" Bill asked.

"No, why should I? I'd just lose."

Bill turned and stared at me. He put his hands on my shoulders and shook his head. "You *are* a loser, Penny Snow, with an attitude like that. I thought I liked you. I really did. From the first time I saw you at the airport, I thought I liked you. You seemed really special. But you're not!" And with that, he turned and left.

Chapter Eight

More than a dozen times that afternoon and evening I thought about telling my mother about Bill and the horrible things he'd said to me, but something stopped me every time.

Actually, I was afraid she'd agree with him. Because, deep down, I knew there was a grain of truth in what he'd said. Finally, I ended up talking to my mother about the other part of our conversation, the part about Grandad.

She was sitting in front of the large round mirror on her dresser, brushing her hair. She turned when she heard me in the doorway.

"Penny, I thought you were in bed."

"I was," I told her. "I just couldn't sleep."

"Sometimes it's hard to get used to the sounds of the ocean," she said, smiling. "But after a while it lulls you to sleep, and you'll miss that sound when you get back home."

"Mom—" I didn't know where to start.

"What's it like, the rest home where Grandad will go after the house is sold?"

"Very orderly," she finally said. "The nurses are extremely careful with the medications. Dr. Dunn told me all about the place when I called him from Ohio months ago. He praised it as one of the best rest homes in the area."

"Have you ever been there?"

She stopped brushing and bent over to remove her bedroom slippers. "Yes, I went with your grandfather the last summer we were here to see one of his friends, and I was very impressed. The place is run on a very rigid schedule. The patients are kept busy and happy. Why, Penny, you seem very worried. Would you like to go and see the place for yourself?" she offered.

"Do they let people like me visit?"

"Certainly," she said, getting up from the bed. "Why not tomorrow? Grandad has an appointment at the home, I think for one-thirty. Bill has promised to drive him over. Seems he has to pick out his room and reserve it. You see, they even give him a choice of rooms, like in a hotel."

I thought of having to see Bill again, actually be in the same car with him. I didn't know how I'd face him after the things he'd said. "Yes. I'd like that," I told my mother. "In fact, I think I'd love that!"

I was thinking rapidly, a whole jumble of thoughts. Sure! That would be great! I was mad at Bill, but definitely didn't want to be enemies with him. Once we saw each other again, I'd explain about my hip, how I could really injure it if I wasn't careful. The day would end up with Bill red-faced and apologizing to me! Besides, I really did want to see the home.

Quickly I kissed my mother good night and started down the hall. She called after me to have a good night's sleep. We would be going up to the attic the next day, and there would be a lot of heavy lugging; so we needed all the rest we could get.

It was a busy morning just like my mother had promised. Even Frankie helped carry dusty objects down from the attic. A few times I got carried away and stopped working to check out some of the things.

"You can have that old jewelry box," Grandad said when he caught me studying it.

"It's all hand carved," I said in wonder.

"Every piece is inlaid wood," he told me.

"After your grandmother died, I put it up here because it hurt me to see it every night. Now it's yours; I'm sure your grandmother would have wanted you to have it."

"Thanks, Grandad," I told him, and I placed a kiss somewhere in the middle of his white hair.

Bill, with a sweatband around his forehead, carried the bigger boxes down from the attic, placing them in the middle of the living room. My mother sat on the floor going through the things, separating the items that would be sold from those she would be shipping home.

Bill kept his eyes from mine, although I tried to catch him looking at me. I wanted to stare him right in the face, show him I was no loser. Maybe he would break down even before our trip to the home and tell me he was sorry for the cruel things he'd said. I waited all morning, but the apology never came. Bill left about eleven-thirty to take his grandmother shopping. He said he'd pick us up for the trip to Ocean View Home at one. He didn't say a word to me.

"Can I go to the old people's home, too?" Frankie asked during lunch.

"It's not an old people's home, Frankie," she told him, placing a glass of milk in front of him. "It's a home for retired senior citizens. And, no, you can't go this time. We're not going to traipse the whole family through. Later, OK."

"It's a crazy house, that's what it is," my grandfather grumbled under his breath. "Everyone there is crazy. If they weren't, they wouldn't be there. That's all I can say."

My mother shook her head and sighed. "Penny can draw her own conclusions," she told him.

My grandfather turned to me and smiled. "I'm sure you will," he said. "But I'd better warn you, honey, it's pretty awful. There are about thirty people, men and women, all put into the living room, and they're told to sit at the card tables, behave themselves, and play chess or bridge, or they'll be locked up in their rooms. When the bell rings, they line up and go from the living room to the dining room for a terribly 'healthy' meal of sawdust and spinach. When the bell rings again, they all line up and go back to playing chess and bridge. Then in comes a nasty old nurse with a spoon and a bottle of green liquid and pills big enough for a horse. Everyone has to take medicine so that they go to sleep soundly. That's so the night nurses aren't disturbed while they're so busy watching TV." Grandad took a sip of the hot coffee my mother had put before him. He ignored her scowls and looked directly at me. "Everything, absolutely everything, is done by the bell. I'll bet if they ever forgot that darn bell, everyone would die in their sleep!"

"That's enough, Dad," my mother told him angrily. "You're saying horrible things."

I put my hand over his for a moment. "Grandad, if it's really so terrible, why don't you just come and stay with us? We have that extra room, and we could have a lot of fun."

My mother stood in the middle of the kitchen, her plate of salad in her hand. Her shoulders drooped, and I knew I'd brought up a painful subject for her. She had pleaded with Grandad so many times.

"Not on your life, my little Penny!" He laughed. "You're just like your mother, nagging me about something I just will not do! I'm part of this state. I love it, and I don't want to leave!"

My mother's eyes met mine, and they said, "You see, Penny. There's nothing much we can do to change things."

We were busy cleaning up the kitchen when Bill knocked on the door. My grandfather opened it, and they exchanged warm greetings. Bill looked over the top of my head and said a polite hello to my mother. Frankie had already gone to Bobby's house, taking Rusty with him.

The three of us headed for the Buick, and my grandfather insisted on sitting in the back. "Sit in the front with Bill," he told me. "Then I can stretch out in the back and put up my feet." I knew he just wanted us to be together. It wouldn't do much good, though, knowing Bill thought I was a loser.

"I wonder what my dad is doing right now," I said, looking back at my grandfather. "It's three hours later there. He must be out in the garden pulling weeds, like my mother told him not to do."

"Sometimes, pulling weeds is good for the soul," he answered. "He can go back to his typewriter afterward and write up a storm."

I smiled fondly at my grandfather. He was such a great old man, so full of fun. I couldn't imagine him in the stuffy place he'd described at lunch. I figured he'd exaggerated a whole lot. He loved to tell wild, overblown stories.

We passed all the familiar houses and

buildings in Newport, then swung onto a side road and began climbing a steep hill. We found the house behind scores of tall pines and maples at the end of a long circular driveway.

"It must be hundreds of years old, a lot older than your house, Grandad," I said.

"They named it Ocean View many years ago because you could actually see a piece of the ocean back then," he told us. "But the trees grew so tall I don't think you could see a tidal wave from any one of those windows now."

As we stepped out of the car, I heard the distant sound of a bell. Grandad and I exchanged glances and broke into laughter. Bill looked at us curiously, and we laughed even harder.

We stepped through the front door, and I followed my grandfather over to a desk where a woman in a nurse's uniform sat bent over a stack of papers. She knew Grandad, smiled at him, and handed him a folder. "Mr. Penfield, so nice to see you on this bright, shining morning. Give this folder to Dr. Sims when he comes out."

A bell rang, and I could hear a lot of shuffling going on in the living room. Grandad and

I looked at each other and again broke up, to Bill's complete confusion.

"Don't mind us, Bill," I told him, still giggling softly. "It's a kind of private joke." A nurse brushed by us, pushing a cart filled with bottles of green liquid and capsules of all colors, and I started to giggle again.

We sat on uncomfortable living room chairs and waited for Grandad's turn with Dr. Sims. First, I watched the old nurse working at her desk, her shiny glasses turning this way and that as she examined the morning mail. Then I watched Bill out of the corner of my eye so that he wouldn't feel me staring at him. He'd picked up an old *Mechanics Illustrated* magazine and thumbed through it. I had to admit he was pretty cute. I loved the way his hair flopped into his eyes.

Restless, I crossed the room and headed for the water cooler. "It's broken, dearie," the nurse with the sparkling glasses called out, "but there's another one upstairs."

I smiled weakly back at her and headed up the staircase. It was just too embarrassing sitting in the same room as Bill, feeling so warmly toward him and knowing how he felt about me. I mean, he hadn't even apologized yet.

Finally I went downstairs and sat down again. The nurse called Grandad's name. "Mr. William Penfield," she said loudly as though the place were packed with people waiting to be called.

"Yes, ma'am," my grandfather answered, clutching the folder to his chest. I watched him open the big oak doors and felt a pang of sadness.

This clearly was not a place for my fun-loving grandfather. Why couldn't we work something out for him? I could understand why he didn't want to leave Newport after living there all his life, why he wouldn't go back with us to Carousel. He'd be pulling up all his roots. At least this way he could go back and look at his old house again sometimes or maybe get Bill to take him for a ride in those cool, green woods. Suppose the people who bought the house tore it down to rebuild—

As though he were reading my mind, Bill turned to me and said, "Penny, I've known your grandfather for a long time. He gave me a summer job taking care of his yard when I first came to Newport. And then when I found out I was going to have to stay on, he made sure he kept me busy so I wouldn't have a lot of time to feel unhappy. I just can't picture him living here. And those pushy nurses making him take all that junk he doesn't need. And the lack of physical exercise. And this whole place seems to be just maintained for these people to die!"

"We've got to think of something," I said urgently.

At that the oak doors parted, and my grandfather appeared, not smiling now. "Dr. Sims said I could have the room in the corner of the west wing, the one in the back, overlooking the parking lot," he said dismally. "There won't be another vacant room in September unless they have a sudden death—" Somehow, my grandfather looked smaller and thinner, and his face was very white, like chalk. "I won't even be able to *try* to see the ocean, stuck away like that in the back of the building."

Bill walked the few feet to the entrance of the living room, where most of the people were sitting at tables playing chess or checkers. "I don't think there is such a thing here as 'sudden death,' " he said coldly. "I think most of them are dead already."

"You're not helping things, Bill," I whispered to him. "You're just plain morbid."

"Don't whisper for my benefit," my grandfather said. "There are a few, as a matter of fact, whom I've met, and they hate it here as much as I'm going to." We headed for the door. "There are twin brothers, Abe and Nat," Grandad told us. "They're absolutely miserable here. They say they'd rather run on the beach until they drop dead than stay up here another ten years playing checkers."

Bill's dark blue eyes stared into mine, and I could almost see his head bubbling with ideas. "Penny, meet me on the bottom steps of the beach stairs tonight after dinner," he whispered.

Chapter Nine

That night, as soon as I saw Bill running along the sand, I grabbed my sweater and walked down the beach steps to meet him. He stood leaning on the stair railing, breathing hard.

"I'm really not through," he told me. "Run the rest of the way with me, Penny. It's only a short distance."

"I can't," I told him. "It would be the very worst thing for me. I'd hurt my leg again." Bill gave me a funny look. "I mean it, Bill. My doctor told me not to overwork my hip," I said annoyed with him now. "Anyway, we were supposed to be talking about my grandfather, not running."

Bill sat down on the bottom step, and I dropped down beside him. "The summer is going by too fast," I told him. "Jason Eddings, the realtor, came by today with a couple who are really serious about the house. My mom said it looks like a sure thing this time."

"Not if your grandfather interferes," he said.

"What do you mean?"

"Actually, it's kind of funny," Bill said, breaking into laughter. "I've watched Jason Eddings knock himself out with a prospective buyer. He gets the house practically sold, and then your grandfather moves in and ruins the sale when Mr. Eddings's back is turned."

"How does he do that?"

I overheard him once when I stopped to rest on this bottom step. He started out with, 'Now, I shouldn't say this, but you seem like good people. I feel I owe it to you to tell you the facts before you buy my place. Ordinarily I wouldn't do this, but as I said, you look like good people . . ."

"My grandfather did that? I don't believe it! He's been trying to sell the place for months now!"

Bill laughed. "I'll bet he's done the same thing a number of times. In his heart he doesn't want to sell the house. He's only following doctor's orders. I'm sure he knows he can't keep it up forever, but at least he's buying himself some more time. And no one can accuse him of not cooperating."

We began to walk slowly along the beach.

"Bill," I said seriously, "I think I may have an idea. It just might be the best thing for Grandad. About three blocks away from my house in Ohio, a Mrs. Green, who owns a big, old house, has turned her home into a boardinghouse since her husband died. Except it's not a regular boardinghouse."

"What do you mean?"

"Well, in a regular boardinghouse people live there who are still working. They eat their meals and sleep there, usually just until they can get situated somewhere else. They choose it over a hotel because they like the family atmosphere."

"And what makes her place different?"

"She only takes in retired folks, who aren't sick enough for rest homes but need some extra care and attention."

"Wow!" Bill exclaimed excitedly. "That kind of place already exists in Ohio? That's amazing because I came up with the same idea myself this afternoon. All this time I thought I was inventing something new!"

"Really, Bill?" I cried. "Then you think it

could be done, too? It would be super with Grandad's view of the ocean and everything."

"That's exactly what I thought!" Bill answered. "They could get a cook, a maid, and a live-in nurse. And I've been thinking for a long time about an exercise program for your grandfather. You know, I've watched him many times on the beach. He loves to walk, and in time I think he could learn to move at a much faster pace, maybe get into jogging."

"Are you crazy?" I said, turning to Bill. "My grandfather is seventy-two, and he's already suffered one heart attack. If the mailman hadn't stopped by and knocked on the kitchen door for him to sign for a package, he might have died all alone!"

"That's the whole point, Penny," Bill said enthusiastically. "I visited a class especially for heart patients. Dr. Terrance had told me about a special class he taught. When I showed an interest, he invited me to visit it in Eugene. I even took my grandparents so that they could see what was being done." There was no way to stop Bill now. "You should have been there, Penny, you would never have believed those people had been seriously ill at one time. Years ago after a heart attack, you spent the rest of your life putting your affairs in order and resting. The result was that you usually died shortly afterward. Now the whole idea is to get your body back in shape or in even better shape than before. I talked to your grandfather, and he told me he used to run. But I think he's a little scared now."

"He has good reason to be," I said. "After all, his heart has been damaged."

"But running actually strengthens the heart. Even the brain is nourished by the supply of oxygen." He leaned down, picked up a stone, and threw it far out into the ocean. "What I'm trying to say is if we really do get this boardinghouse going, I could help with a light exercise program."

"We've got to talk to Grandad about the idea," I told Bill.

"Let me be there when you tell him," he said. Then suddenly, he stopped walking and turned to me. "Penny, how long will it be before you'll do something like running?"

"Maybe never."

"Is it really that bad?"

"Yes," I said coldly.

"Penny," Bill said gently, "isn't it that you won't run?"

"I told you just a little while ago I might injure myself all over again if I do too much."

"Is that what your doctor said?"

"Sort of. You know, Bill, I was good at sports. Very good. But if I tried swimming or tennis now, I'd never be terrific at them again."

"And you wouldn't want to play those sports unless you were the best?"

"I've got to go now, Bill," I said, turning toward the house. "I only came out to talk about my grandfather, not me."

"Will you try running with me sometime?" he persisted.

"No," I said and looked away from him. "I guess I'll see you tomorrow. Come over early so that we can tell my mother and grandfather about our idea."

Bill stood up and walked over to me. He looked deeply into my eyes, and all of a sudden I felt as if he could read my thoughts. "Maybe next time you'll run with me, Penny. I'll just keep asking you until you give in."

"Don't hold your breath," I said and smiled. "I'll never do it. See you tomorrow—early."

Bill started the run in the direction of his house. Then he turned back to me. "Penny," he called, "my grandmother always says, 'Never say never.' "

Chapter Ten

Bill appeared at the kitchen door the next morning just as we were finishing breakfast. By that time I was absolutely bursting, I wanted so badly to tell everyone about our boardinghouse idea. "Don't anyone get up!" I ordered the group at the kitchen table. "Pull up a chair, Bill, I haven't said a word yet."

"Did someone win the lottery?" Grandad asked.

"No, better than that," I told him.

Then Bill and I began, our words tumbling out excitedly. My grandfather sat back in his chair and listened carefully. My mother held her coffee cup halfway to her mouth the whole time, but the coffee never reached her lips. "Dad," she said after we'd finished, "have you ever thought of anything like that?"

My grandfather stroked his chin. "At one time I thought of hiring a companion. But I worried that I might get someone in here I didn't like. Then I'd have to fire him, which I wouldn't like, and then hire someone else. But I never thought of running a real business. With all the bedrooms we have here, it could certainly be done."

"You'd still have privacy when you needed it, but when you felt lonely, you could be surrounded by friends."

"It would take a permit," my grandfather said.

"And a lot of redecorating," my mother added, glancing around. "The cooking wouldn't be easy because older people need to have special diets. We'd have to improve the kitchen. Then there are the bedrooms."

"I'd help," Bill offered.

"My own retirement home," my grandfather said, closing his eyes for a moment. Then he opened them and smiled at all of us. "It would be a dream come true. I wouldn't ever have to sell this place—"

My mother was smiling, too. Bill and I exchanged glances. We had solved the problem!

"Wow, then we could come back out and see you and Rusty again," Frankie said.

"Oh, Grandad, think how great it would

be. You could make your own rules. You wouldn't have to have bells all the time."

"We could sit out on the sun porch and see the ocean and the sunsets," grandfather added.

"But there would be some rules," my mother said, her brow wrinkling like it always does when she's worried. "It couldn't be just a fun house where you'd eat whatever you wanted and ignore doctor's orders."

"Why can't he have a fun house?" Frankie asked seriously, and we all laughed.

"I know," Grandad said. "I wouldn't do that to the other boarders. They'll be putting their trust in me; so I'll take good care of them." My mother looked relieved.

Bill suggested his exercise plan. Grandad listened quietly, and when Bill was finished, he got up and went over to the sink for a glass of water. Turning to face us, he said, "Looks like you kids have been giving my problem a lot of serious thought. Now, I've been reading about such health programs, and I hear they really help. Let me offer you the first position at Grandad Penfield's Home," he joked. "Part-time, of course, because you've got to keep up your grades at school."

The plans were beginning to form. That

morning we sat at the kitchen table for three hours plotting what we'd have to do to turn the house into a boarding home. Frankie left after a little while to go over to Bobby's, but the rest of us were too engrossed in the idea to move. My mother brought out paper and pencils, and we jotted down all the necessary changes that would have to be made on the house.

We figured there should be two people in each bedroom, except for my grandfather's. The house would be open to married couples as well as single folks. Grandad thought right away of the twin brothers he'd met at Ocean View, who he was sure would love to come. He remembered the Gunther sisters, too. "I love the thought of stealing business from that place." Grandad smiled mischievously.

"Ocean View won't be too upset," my mother told him. "They have a long waiting list. You won't hurt their business at all."

"Darn," my grandfather said. But he still kept on smiling.

My mother made a phone call to Dr. Dunn while we still huddled around the kitchen table. We were talking about the pool table my grandfather had decided to put down on his list. Mom talked to the doctor for a long time and smiled through most of the conversation. "He's agreed to do it," she said, putting down the phone at last. "He told me he wants to go into semiretirement himself; so he's now in the process of sending most of his patients to a younger doctor. This could be a great thing for him. He's agreed to visit your home on a weekly basis and be on call, of course."

My grandfather's eyes sparkled. "It seems like it's going to work out."

"All the stuff we packed." I moaned a little.

"We would have had to clean out this place to make room for the boarders anyway," my grandfather told me. "The only things I want unpacked are those tools of mine."

There would be a lot to do. My mother called the realtor and told him that we were taking the house off the market. Bill and I headed for the garage to unpack the tools. Everything was looking up.

The phone rang while Bill and I were out in the garage. Mom yelled out to me, and I ran in to take the call on the sun porch.

"Penny, you won't believe it! Ron asked me out, you know that cute lifeguard I told you about? I want you to meet him! Can you come over to the pool tomorrow about one?"

I was going to say no, but it suddenly hit

me that it would be fun to meet the guy Giddy liked. I really wanted to see Giddy and Jan again. "I'll come," I told her, laughing. "I'd love to come!"

We said goodbye, and even after I put the phone down, I heard her tinkling laughter in my head. She sounded as if she really liked Ron.

I went out to the garage again and opened up one of the boxes. Bill was already hanging tools back on hooks. "That was Giddy," I explained.

"Giddy Jones, I know her from school," he answered.

"She wants me to come to the city pool tomorrow and meet a guy she likes."

"I thought you were avoiding the pool."

"Well—"

"Would you like me to go with you?" Bill asked with concern.

I almost dropped the pliers I was holding. "That would be great—but I'm not going to swim, just meet Ron and maybe see Giddy and Jan at work."

"Terrific, I'll go with you." I was glad Bill knew my friends. He seemed to like them. And having a little moral support from him would be just great. It would be hard to watch everyone swimming and know I never could again.

"Maybe we could stop by for some pizza at Gallucci's after we visit your friends," Bill offered as we stacked the empty boxes into the corner.

"Great, I love that place!" I looked down at my filthy hands, and when I looked up, Bill was staring at me. All these warm feelings I'd had at Ocean View came back to me in a flash. *Stop it, Penny Snow,* I told myself. *Remember, this guy thinks you're a loser!*

Chapter Eleven

"I'm sorry, Penny, but you can't run off this afternoon unless you take Frankie along," Mom said, breaking the bad news to me. "Your grandfather and I have a busy schedule. We have to see about a business license, pick out wallpaper for the bedrooms, and meet with Dr. Dunn. He wants to introduce us to a married couple, who are already interested in moving into your grandfather's house."

"You mean he has boarders already?" Bill exclaimed.

"This old place will fill up quickly," Grandad told Bill proudly. "I called those twin brothers over at Ocean View this morning, and they're so excited I'm afraid they'll have strokes before they can move in here in September!"

"We *have* to take Frankie?" I moaned. "Can't he tag along with you or go over to Bobby's for a few hours?"

My mother gave me an exasperated look. "I can't imagine dragging Frankie along to do all those chores, and you know Bobby's family left this morning for a few days."

"I don't want to go with you either, Penny!" Frankie broke in. "Mom, I don't mind staying in the house alone."

"Absolutely not!" Mom said sternly, and I knew she meant it. *Oh, well, it hadn't really been a formal date—*

"It's OK, Mrs. Snow," Bill told her. "We don't mind."

"Speak for yourself," I whispered to him as we left the kitchen.

We had the miserable chore that morning of peeling off the old wallpaper. My grandfather could save a lot of money if the old paper was off before the paperhanger came.

We decided to do all the upstairs rooms first. My grandfather had rented a funny-looking steam contraption to help get the hard parts off. I was to tackle my own room, Frankie and Bill would do Frankie's room, and my mother would start on hers the next day, since she'd be spending most of that day running errands with my grandfather.

Since the wallpaper was very old, most of it peeled off easily. In fact, it was kind of fun to do. I hated to tear off the paper in my room, but it had to be done. I picked up my sponge and started to soak the corner of one strip. I found it came off neatly. When I realized I could pull off a huge piece at a time, I began to work even more carefully. If I could peel off a section without tearing it, I'd be able to put a series of the pictures together and maybe frame them when I got home.

When my mother came in to say goodbye and to see how I was doing, she laughed at my slow progress. "You'll have to work much faster than that."

"I will, after I get one of each picture."

"You're going to save it?"

"Yes. It would be a beautiful souvenir."

Mom stood and watched as I carefully lifted off a whole picture. "I grew up with this paper. My best friend and I would come up here and share our secrets in this room. We often thought of those girls on the paper and wondered why they had that sad look when they parted in the last picture. It was many years before we understood."

"Where is she now?"

"Actually, Penny, I don't even know. We both left home to go to college. I heard she married and went to Florida. I settled in Ohio with your father, and we lost touch."

"How sad," I commented.

"It is. But I'll always remember her when I think of this wallpaper. Now, I have to get going with your grandfather. See you later."

I studied the pictures for a moment before I continued peeling. They would make a lovely Christmas present for Mom.

Newport municipal pool was jumping with kids. The noise was deafening, but it didn't seem to be bothering those kids. I glanced around, looking for my friends, and found Jan waiting for me by the front counter. She looked a little surprised to see Bill. I'd never mentioned that I knew him. The pool hadn't changed much since I'd seen it a few years before—still crowded and noisy, and wonderfully fun. Giddy waved to me from the bleachers, and I went over to her. She was sitting beside a guy who, by the way she looked at him and smiled, had to be Ron. He was a little shorter than Bill and had reddish-blond hair, gray eyes, a wide smile, and a great tan. Giddy introduced him as Newport High's star football player, and he looked embarrassed.

Wow! I thought, *Ron sure is good looking, and he seems perfect for Giddy.* I smiled at him, but I don't think he saw me because he only had eyes for Giddy.

We all sat down on the bleachers, except Frankie. He spent the whole time crawling from one bench to another. I guess it was pretty boring for him, just the bunch of us talking.

I watched the kids swimming, and from my perch I spied two little girls trying the butterfly stroke. A sudden ache shot through me. I longed to jump in beside them. Maybe if there were no spectators or other swimmers, if I could just have that big pool to myself . . .

"What are you thinking about?" Bill whispered in my ear.

"Nothing special," I told him, trying to smile.

"I don't believe you," he said, squeezing my hand gently. "This must be hard for you."

I shrugged and tried to smile again. I couldn't believe he was being so understanding.

I had a great time talking with Giddy and Jan. Ron turned out to be as nice as he was good-looking. Pretty soon, though, Bill and I got hungry and decided to head over to

Gallucci's. I'd spent enough time watching other people swim, too.

"I wish we could come with you," Jan said, "but we have to be here until three this afternoon."

Giddy waved a quick goodbye, then jumped into the deep end to stop two small boys who were having a watery fistfight. Ron excused himself and went after a little girl who was making a game out of running around the wet outskirts of the pool.

"You see, they keep us on our toes—and wet!" Jan said and giggled. "We're responsible for everyone's safety, and that doesn't make us popular, believe me!"

"But you seem like you're having fun," I answered wistfully.

"I am," Jan answered. Her smile let me know that she had heard the wistful tone in my voice. "Listen, I'll call you soon, OK?"

But I knew she wouldn't and Giddy wouldn't have time to see me, either. Between their jobs and their boyfriends, it would be awfully hard to squeeze me in.

I found Frankie, and Bill and I dragged him toward the door. I took one last look at the pool before we left. Everyone was having such a good time. But I just didn't fit in with them anymore.

"The best pizza in town!" Bill told us as he turned on the ignition.

"I remember it that way," I said.

"Hey, let's go out to the old spooky lighthouse! We could get our pizza to go," Frankie suggested from the backseat.

"Can't," Bill said. "I've got to cut the grass at my house, and then I promised my grandfather I'd start refinishing his boat."

"Rats!" Frankie said bitterly. "The summer will be gone, and I'll miss the whole thing."

"No, you won't," I said. "We'll manage to get the time somehow, later on. Just be patient."

Grumbling, Frankie peered out the window. "No, we won't. I know we won't!"

"Have you ever been out to the lighthouse?" Bill asked me.

"Sure," I told him, "but it was years ago. I didn't even know it was still there anymore."

"Oh, it's still there all right. The people of Newport have made sure that it will be, too. Last year they banded together and got it declared a historical landmark. We'll take

Frankie there sometime." Bill pulled the car into the parking lot behind Gallucci's.

"Oh, please, please, please," Frankie shrieked in my ear.

"Frankie, stop screaming," I said as we got out of the car and walked into Gallucci's.

Bill ordered a pizza with everything on it. "Listen, Frankie," he said as we waited for our pie. "I really can't take you out there today, but I'll tell you the story. See, the lighthouse was built back in eighteen seventy-one to warn sailors out on the ocean on foggy days. After a more modern lighthouse was built at Yaquina Head, the old one was never lit again. It seems that it's haunted by a ghost—, a girl, about sixteen or so, named Muriel. There's a path leading up from the beach to the lighthouse on the cliffs, and a few people swear they've seen her walking on it."

"Wow!" Frankie said. I knew he'd heard my grandfather tell it before, but he still seemed impressed.

"Way back when Newport was just a very small town, a sloop sailed across the bar. The crew and her skipper had bad reputations, and the townspeople who saw the sloop sail in were a little scared at first. A boat was lowered, and a man about forty years of age and a girl were rowed ashore. The man asked the people if he could leave his daughter with a family in Newport for about two weeks. The rough seas had been too much for her, he said, and she needed to be ashore. A woman in the crowd said she'd be glad to have Muriel, and so the father sailed away."

"And just left her?" Frankie slumped down on his chair. "My dad wouldn't do that."

"Yep, just sailed away! Anyhow, Muriel got very depressed when a whole month went by and her father hadn't returned for her. Then in August she happened to meet a group of teenagers, and she was happy to be with people her own age. The group decided to visit the deserted lighthouse. They got the key from a man who had been put in charge of the place. Muriel didn't want to go, but one boy in the group, Harold Welch, finally convinced her to. See, Muriel and the boy were kind of falling-in-love."

"Yuck!" Frankie said. "Grandad never said anything about them loving each other."

"Well, I don't want to ruin it for you, kid," Bill told him, laughing, "but that's how I heard the story."

"It's getting to the scary stuff," Frankie

said, with a little shiver. "I like the scary parts!"

"The kids entered the old lighthouse, investigated the many rooms, climbed the stairs to the second floor, and even found a small landing with a tiny room off on one side."

"Did the ghost jump out then?"

"No, no," Bill said. "Wait, you're ahead of my story. It was a linen closet, with shelves and drawers, but one wall was made of heavy sheet iron. When they pushed it back, they could peer down into a deep well. Something happened to the weather then—"

"The scary part," Frankie whispered.

"The sunny afternoon became misty, and the whole world turned gray. Well, the group gladly left the old house. It was getting a little creepy when the fog started to roll in, but just as they were leaving, Muriel insisted that she would have to run back because she'd dropped her handkerchief somewhere in the house."

"But why would she go back for a dumb thing like that?" Frankie's eyes were wide with fright now.

"I don't know," Bill said. "Maybe it was fine lace or something. Anyway, they say that Harold wanted to go with her, but she insisted it would take her only a second. He stood out there waiting for her while the rest of the group ran on ahead, but the wait got longer and longer, and she never returned—"

"Oh, wow!" Frankie said.

"Sometime later Harold called the group back and they reentered the house to search for her. And here is the terrible part—upstairs on the landing they found a pool of warm, red blood. In the linen closet they picked up a blood-stained handkerchief. But that's not all—the panel in the wall had been replaced, and no matter how they tried, they could not open it. They never found another trace of Muriel, and the sloop with her father never came back."

The pizza arrived just then. We dug in and ate every slice. Then we paid the bill and walked out to the car. "But you never really finished the story," Frankie said as we pulled away from Gallucci's. "What about the *real* scary part!"

"Not much more to tell, Frankie, except that people who visit the lighthouse area in heavy fog claim they hear a moaning sound, like the cry of someone in pain, and even sometimes a cry for help. Sailors in ships passing in the night claim they see a light burning in the tower."

"And there isn't any?" Frankie asked breathlessly.

"And there isn't any."

"Wow!" Frankie said, throwing himself on the backseat. "I want to go there more than anything!"

"It's just a story, a legend," Bill said, turning the corner and heading for the traffic light. "I wouldn't want you to have bad dreams about it."

"Don't forget your promise," Frankie reminded him.

"I won't," Bill said. "Someday I'll take you there."

"That's what grown-ups always say," Frankie said, sitting back on his seat. "And someday never comes!"

Chapter Twelve

"How did it get to be July already?" my mother asked, sipping her frosty lemonade out on the sun porch.

My grandfather kicked off his shoes, wiggled his toes in his socks, and leaned as far back as he could in the wicker rocker. "When you work hard, time goes by quickly," he answered.

He wasn't kidding when he said we'd worked hard. Taking down all that old wallpaper sure wasn't a picnic, and neither was painting all the trim before the wallpaper hanger came. Every day we were completely wiped out by the afternoon.

But every evening, toward sunset, I'd see Bill running, no matter how tired he was. After that day at the pizza place, he'd never asked me out again, but I hoped I knew why. There just wasn't much time left in our days.

And on weekends he'd go out with his grandfather on their boat, and I wouldn't see him at all.

I did get to see Giddy and Jan a bit, but they were so busy with their jobs at the pool, it wasn't that often. Some days I sat around, waiting for the phone to ring. I had to admit I was kind of lonely.

But I had patience, and pretty soon it paid off. On July third Bill asked me if I'd like to see the fireworks with him the next evening. "They're shot off over Yaquina Bay from the Southbeach side," he told me.

"I remember," I said. "I'd like to go with you. Usually our whole family goes together, but with Dad not here, things are a little different. Frankie's already invited Bobby. They can go with my mom and grandad."

Bill's smile broadened. "It's about time we had a few minutes alone," he said, and I could feel the color coming to my face.

During the day on the Fourth, my mom, Frankie, and I went hiking in the pines, then had a picnic on the beach with my grandfather.

That evening Bill picked me up just as the sun, round and scarlet, was beginning to settle comfortably into the ocean. Mom had packed us a supper of fried chicken left over from our picnic, apples, and Cokes, and I'd thrown in Jessica's licorice sticks. We jumped into the Bug and were off.

Bill parked his car on a deserted hill, and I thought we'd definitely be alone. But as the sun disappeared into the ocean, a few more cars trickled in, and before we knew it, we were surrounded by cars, pickups piled high with kids, and even a few joggers.

"We might just as well have brought Frankie along," I told Bill.

"Oh, he's not so bad," Bill said, laughing. "I'm sorry, Penny, I didn't know the whole town of Newport would decide to watch it from the same place!"

After eating we rested our heads on the backs of our seats, knowing we had to wait. Actually I was glad Frankie hadn't come with us. Even if we were surrounded by other people, at least we could talk privately in the car.

You know, I don't think I've ever had such a good time waiting for anything in my life. Bill and I never ran out of things to talk about. Not only was he interesting, he was also a good listener.

At last the fireworks started. Oohs and

aahs burst from the surrounding cars as each spray went up. The bursts and crackles and fiery lights burned through the dark sky. The moon slipped behind a cloud, and I laughed, thinking that maybe the blasts had scared it away.

When Newport had exhausted its supply of fireworks, the cars around us began pulling out. We sat in silence watching them leave, and after about fifteen minutes the hill was deserted except for the yellow Bug with Bill and me safely inside. The moon had disappeared, leaving the sky so black and cluttered with dark rain clouds that I could spot only one star.

"Maybe that's a wishing star," Bill said after a while.

"Was it the first one out tonight?"

"I'm sure it was," Bill said, putting his arm around me. "And you know what I wish? That tonight would go on and on forever." Then he reached over and tilted my head back. He drew me close, and his lips met mine. It was a long, perfect kiss.

But the best part came at the very end.

"I think I'm falling in love with you, Penny," Bill whispered in my ear.

At that particular moment I could have sworn Newport had found some more fireworks and that those rockets were bursting brightly in the sky over Yaquina Bay.

Chapter Thirteen

"Four straight days of rain. I could scream!" my mother said as we were putting away the dishes. It had been raining since the Fourth of July, and everyone was feeling caged in. A person can play backgammon, cards, and Monopoly just so long before getting very bored.

"At least we have plenty of work to do inside," I told her. "But Bill says it sure is holding up the outside painting."

"That boy!" my mother said, shaking her head. "He's really dedicated to his running!" Bill hadn't let the rain change his evening habit. I watched him running in the hardest downpours I'd ever seen. He even looked like he was enjoying it."

"It helps keep him fit," my grandfather said. "I'm looking forward to the day Dr. Dunn lets me do some real running, instead of my walking program."

"Bill has already stepped up your pace,"

Mom said. "Don't rush it. When the doctor tells Bill it's OK, then you can attempt the running."

"Will you run in the rain, too?" Frankie asked. He picked up a piece of paper money from the Monopoly game and began to fold it.

"Stop that!" my mother warned him. "No, your grandfather is not going to run in the rain if I have any say about it."

My grandfather just smiled. "Louise, how about going down to buy one of those machines, those video game things, to attach to the television. I planned to get one for my boarders anyhow. If I buy it early, then I can get really good at the games and maybe win a few side bets with the old geezers."

And that's how I got stuck watching Frankie. First he pestered me to play race car driver with him. Then the sun came out, and he nagged me to take him somewhere.

"The rain might have stopped," I told him, "but it's still pretty soggy out there."

"Call Bill," Frankie whined. "We could all go over to the lighthouse and see if we can hear that scary crying and moaning."

"He's spending the day with his grandfather," I told him, cleaning up the rest of the race cars.

Frankie scowled. "Take me yourself."

"I've only been there once. I wouldn't even remember how to get there because I was a little girl when Grandad took me."

"Was it scary? Did you hear that crying and stuff?"

"I don't remember."

Frankie looked at me as though I were hopeless. "You're dumb, you know that," he said as he ran up the stairs to his room.

"Clean it up while you're up there sulking!" I called after him.

The phone rang; it was Giddy. I propped myself up on a couple of throw pillows on the sun porch swing, a perfect place for a long phone conversation. We finally said goodbye almost an hour later. I lowered the phone to the floor and pushed my head deeper into the pillows. The sun filtered through the tiny panes of glass, warming my face. My eyes drifted closed, only for a few moments, I thought, but when I finally opened them again, I knew it had been much longer. Another hour, at least, had gone by.

My mother and grandfather had, no doubt, stopped to see one of his old friends. They often did on the way home from one of their shopping sprees; so I really wasn't concerned about them. I figured Frankie was busy playing in his room. But when I peeked in, Frankie's room was empty.

I called his name, but the only answer was deadly silence. Checking my bedroom, my mother's, the two across the hall, and all the closets, I left the upstairs and headed for the kitchen. That's what he was doing, I thought, eating as usual and not answering my calls just to annoy me. But the kitchen was empty, too. By now I was beginning to worry. I checked the garage. No Frankie. *He's got to be outside enjoying the sunshine,* I thought to myself. I dashed down the beach stairs only to find an empty beach, not even a sea gull. By the time I'd walked back up the stairs, I could hear my mother and grandfather on the sun porch.

"Where's Frankie?" my grandfather asked excitedly. "Wait until he sees the gadgets I've bought! He's going to love them!"

"I don't know," I confessed. "He went up to his room, and Giddy called, and after her call I fell asleep on the swing. When I got up, I couldn't find him—"

"You couldn't find him?" My mother frowned.

My grandfather looked puzzled. "Well, I

think we'd better locate him. I heard on the car radio that another big storm's brewing, one of the worst yet, and it'll be here within a half hour or so."

The sun still shone through the sun porch. "They must be wrong. It'll hit somewhere else," I told him. "The sun is shining beautifully now."

"They aren't wrong, Penny," he said, putting his arm around me. "Believe me, honey, it's coming. So let's see where your brother is hiding out. Rusty, here, boy," he called. "Gone, too," he said with concern. He rummaged around in the hall closet for a second and pulled out his yellow slicker. In another minute he pulled on his high boots.

"Where are you going?" my mother demanded.

"Out," he told her, gently shoving her out of the way.

"Not without me, you're not," she insisted, going to the closet for her own raincoat and boots.

He found them before she did. "Your boots," he told her, and I could almost see the two of them as they must have been many years before: my mother, the spunky little girl, my grandfather, tall and stubborn, telling his daughter to put her boots on. She grabbed them from him and immediately shoved her feet in them.

"But you two look crazy!" I told them, laughing. "The sun is still shining."

At that moment I heard a familiar sound, the gentle patter of raindrops, and the light slowly dimmed as clouds rolled across the sky.

"I have a funny feeling, Penny," Mom said. "Can you call Bill and ask him to help us look? If we don't find Frankie in the next half hour, it could be serious. I heard the reports of this storm coming in."

"Which way are you and Grandad going? Bill and I can go the other way."

"We'll cover from the Bennet house down to Ship's Hardware where he likes to play Pac-Man."

"But it's just after five. Ship's Hardware has closed."

"I know," she said irritably. "I would just have called the store if they hadn't been."

"I hope he didn't go too far," Grandad said as he followed my mother out the door.

The rain started coming down harder, and it was as dark as if night had suddenly hit Newport. Angry clouds raced in from the ocean, gathering together ready to invade the seacoast town. Grabbing the phone, I dialed Bill's number. He answered on the second ring, and I breathed a sigh of relief. "What's wrong, Penny?" He knew by my voice that something bad had happened.

"I hope nothing," I told him. "Frankie's disappeared. Maybe he took a walk on the beach. He loves to look for strange things, shells and stuff. We're just a little worried because of the storm. Mom and Grandad took off in one direction, and they want us to go in the other."

"Be right there," Bill said, and I heard the phone click.

I threw on my warmest jacket and topped it with my raincoat. The hood would keep my head dry. Frantically I searched around in my closet for my boots. They were hiding behind a box. Thank goodness I'd made room in my suitcase for them. I remembered the day I'd tried to leave them out so that I could bring an extra pair of jeans and some of my favorite shirts. My mother had caught me before I could lock the suitcase.

In minutes Bill was banging on the sun porch door, flashlight in hand. He had run down the beach since it was the fastest way to my grandfather's house. A sudden crack of thunder and a bolt of lightning crashed through the sky just as I opened the door. "Penny, I guarantee Bill Davis's Missing Persons Agency will find your little brother for you," Bill said, giving my hand a squeeze. "Why don't you just stay here, and I'll—"

"No," I interrupted. "If my mother and grandfather are out there in the storm, I'll be there, too. I'm not that much of a loser."

Bill looked down at me, buttoned up the top button of my raincoat, and said, "I'm sorry about that, Penny. You know I didn't mean it." A sudden crack of thunder and a bolt of lightning jolted us back to the present. "Come on," he said. "Be careful on the wooden beach steps. They'll be pretty slippery."

In minutes we were headed up the beach. Bill aimed his flashlight up toward the cliffs, then swung it in an arc, covering the whole beach. Soon we were both hoarse from calling out for Frankie.

"We'll search for a while, but then we've really got to call the police," Bill told me. "We don't want too much time to pass in a storm like this."

Bill, holding my hand, practically dragged me along beside him. He started walking faster and faster, and I had to run a little to stay by his side. Finally, we *were* running, not fast, but faster than walking. We jogged along, stopping to search the darkest parts of the cliffs where Frankie might have fallen over an old log or debris brought in by the pounding waves.

"He wouldn't have gone near the water, would he?" Bill asked, his eyes wide now.

"Definitely not. Frankie is a little afraid of the water. He's heard Grandad tell some wild stories; so I don't think we have to worry about that."

Bill stopped for a few moments while I caught my breath. "Wait," he said. "Just a minute. I think I've got it! The lighthouse! I'm sure of it. He wanted to go so badly. I bet he decided not to wait any longer, and he took Rusty with him!"

"Oh, no," I said, really alarmed now. "But it's so far away!"

"I want you to turn back now," Bill said. "I'll go on alone. We'll stop at the Nortons' house and get another flashlight, and you can take mine on your way back. There's no need for both of us to go that far."

"No," I told him firmly. "He's my brother, and I want to be there if he needs help. And I'm positive you're right about the lighthouse. Oh, why didn't we take him? We were all so busy with our own little problems."

"This is no time to feel guilty," Bill said. "Let's save our breath for running."

I ran as fast as I could alongside Bill, huffing and puffing all the way. Finally we could see the old lighthouse up on the cliff. It seemed close, but it wasn't.

The rain had stopped now, and a heavy fog started rolling in. I found myself climbing the cliffs with Bill, who had to pull me over the slippery rocks. Then we really were close enough to touch the old house.

Suddenly we heard cries.

"He *is* here!" I called out to Bill. "Did you hear that?"

"I sure did. Now all we have to do is find him." We both began calling Frankie's name again. We even called Rusty.

Then Bill fell over something in the path, and we heard a small moan. There he was, sprawled under the bushes, half covered by soaked leaves. He was drenched to the skin, and his right foot was twisted at a funny angle.

Out of the bushes Rusty flew at us as though we might want to hurt Frankie. He barked wildly, trying to protect his friend.

Then he recognized us, whined, and settled back under the bushes.

"It's OK, boy, it's OK, Rusty, boy," Bill said, trying to pat his head. Rusty pulled away, whimpering a little. We knelt down beside Frankie.

My brother's face was smeared with dirt and streaked with tears. "I think I broke my ankle," he said. "I slipped on the walk and fell, and it really hurts."

"You're going to stay right here with Penny and Rusty," Bill said. "I'll go get help so that we don't hurt your ankle more by moving it the wrong way."

I looked up at Bill, and I was really scared now. "You're going to leave us in this place?"

"You'll be OK," he said, smiling. "It will only take me a few minutes, and I'll be back with some help."

Bill ran down toward the beach, and the fog swallowed him up. I tried my best to console Frankie. I took off my warm jacket from under my raincoat, and I wrapped it around him. Rusty whined on and on, and I felt as if we three were the only creatures left in the world. The old house seemed to moan and creak along with the wind and the fog. The minutes turned into a half hour. I shivered. I wished that I had something to wrap around poor Rusty.

I stood up and stretched my legs. Funny, my hip didn't hurt after all that running! Stooping down again to Frankie, I said, "Bill will be back soon. Then, in just a short time you'll be home drinking hot chocolate with Mom and Grandad."

"But I think my ankle is broke—really broke," Frankie said and whimpered.

I swallowed hard. "Then just a quick trip to the hospital will do it," I said, trying to comfort him. "No problem, it will heal."

"But you never healed," Frankie said and moaned.

"Oh, yes, I did, Frankie," I told him, standing up again. "See, I was running tonight with Bill when we were trying to find you. I was OK all along, but I didn't know it until tonight."

Slowly the fog started to lift, and by the time Bill came back with an ambulance, which had driven along the old road running along the top of the cliff, the night was clear again. You never would have guessed there had been a terrible storm. I rode in the back with Frankie and an attendant. Bill and Rusty sat up front with the driver. "It was a good thing you called out to us when you did," I told Frankie as we drove up to the hospital. "The fog was so bad we never would have found you."

"But I didn't call out," he told me. For a moment I couldn't say anything.

"Are you sure you didn't, not even once?" I asked, my voice shaking.

"I'm sure," he said, "because I didn't think anyone was around to hear me. I was just kind of waiting for the pain to stop so that I could limp over to someone's house. But it was kind of funny, I thought someone else was out there, too, hurt like me, because I heard a moaning sound. Like someone calling for help."

I called my mother and grandfather, who had just gotten back to the house. They arrived at the hospital completely soaked. Frankie had broken his ankle and would have to stay in the hospital for a few days. Mom cried for a long time, but Grandad was wonderful. He assured her that everything would be OK.

Later Bill and I sat in our living room, talking and drinking hot chocolate in front of a fire Grandad had built in the fireplace.

"I guess the old lighthouse will always be a

mystery," I said after telling him that Frankie had not called out. "Maybe there really is a ghost. I'd certainly believe it after tonight."

"There's even a greater mystery than that," Bill said and smiled at me. "The mystery is that you can't run—but I saw tonight what a good runner you are!"

He just wouldn't let up on me, and he didn't leave that night until I promised I'd go running with him the next day.

Chapter Fourteen

I had to stand on a footstool to reach my running shoes on the top shelf of the closet. One of the first things I'd done when I unpacked my bags was to push them as far to the back of the shelf as I could. I thought of Jessica and could almost see her smiling as I got them down and slipped them on. They looked great. My clock said 5:30 A.M., and I shuddered to think that instead of sleeping in, I was going jogging. Why had I agreed to such a dumb thing?

"Just for a little way," Bill had urged me. "Just up to the Norton place and back, and I won't ask for more, I promise."

Anything to shut him up, I thought as I laced the shoes. He had told me to have only a glass of orange juice. "Eat a full breakfast when you get back," he'd warned, "not before." I never ate too much for breakfast, anyhow, so I didn't mind.

I wore my most comfortable pair of cutoffs and my dark blue sweatshirt. "It will seem very cold that early in the morning," Bill had told me, "but don't dress too warmly. Your body will generate a lot of heat when you start running. And it doesn't matter what you look like, just that you're comfortable."

After I drank my orange juice, I heard a faint knock on the sun porch door. Bill stood there in a dark green T-shirt and cutoffs, grinning widely at me. "You didn't think I'd make it, did you?" I asked, smiling back at him.

"You look great," he told me.

I just grinned. "Shhh—don't wake Grandad or Mom. After last night they need their rest!"

"Let's take Rusty," Bill whispered. "He'll enjoy the run." We turned from the house and walked down the beach stairs. "You've never run before?" Bill asked.

"No, not really. And I'm not so sure I should be doing it now."

"But you own running shoes."

"New, never used, a present from my best friend. But I'm not really supposed to use them."

"I checked with your mother quite awhile

ago," he said, "and she told me your doctor had actually *urged* you to get some exercise. So don't hand me that story about it being bad for your leg."

I stopped short. Rude! He was absolutely, totally rude! "You're calling me a liar now!"

"No," Bill said, his face getting red. "Maybe you believed that story yourself, actually convinced yourself that it was true. That way you don't have to worry about competition or winning."

"Forget it—just forget the whole thing! I'm not going running with you, Bill Davis," I yelled.

He stood between me and the steps so I couldn't run back to the house. I turned the other way and almost fell over Rusty but continued my dash down the beach. Bill was right behind me. "Penny, wait," he called. "I didn't mean—" But I kept going. "No, Penny! Don't run on your toes. You'll get sore calf muscles and strain your tendons!"

Then I started to laugh. I just couldn't help myself. Throwing myself down on the sand, I laughed harder than I had in a long time. Bill threw himself down beside me, laughing, too, and I swear that even Rusty was smiling.

"Oh, Penny," Bill said. "I didn't mean to make you mad at me again. That's the last thing I'd ever want to do—because I love you!" Slowly he leaned over and kissed me full on my lips, a very firm kiss that left me as breathless as though I'd been running for miles.

"OK, that's enough fooling around," he exclaimed suddenly, pulling me to my feet. "Let's get on with the running!" I laughed again and stood up. "What I want you to do, Penny, is listen to your body. Really listen," he told me. "Ask yourself if your leg or hip *really* hurts when you run gently. If you're feeling pain, then your body is telling you not to run. Maybe we could fix that with exercises. But if your body doesn't protest, we'll run!"

He leaned over and brushed my forehead with a light kiss. "Remember, your goal is just to run. You're not trying to outdistance anybody." He stood beside me, close enough to touch me. "Now breathe naturally. If you're running slowly, you won't need to open your mouth too wide, but as you move faster, don't be afraid to gulp in all the air you can get." We started running on the firm part of the sand. "Keep your body straight, head up. Lean slightly forward."

"What do I do with my arms? They seem so awkward."

"Keep your elbows bent, but not held tightly against your body. Keep your hands relaxed."

We were running at a good pace now, Rusty dashing off in front of us. My body didn't ache anywhere, and I had to admit I was surprised. I listened carefully for any signs from my body, and there was nothing except a feeling of wanting to go on and on.

"We'll run for just a short distance," Bill said. "Then we'll rest up near the cliff by the Norton house."

I could feel my stride smoothing out a little, and in a few minutes I was sweating. *Next time I'll wear just a T-shirt,* I thought. I had a feeling of real control for the first time since the accident. When I walked, I always babied my bad hip. Now, with running, I just flowed along naturally.

When we reached the cliffs under the Norton house, Bill touched my arm gently. "Let's rest here," he said. "Run in place for a few seconds to warm down before you rest."

Rusty had run right past us, but not for long. When he saw we were not going to join him, he came running back. The three of us scooted over to lean against the cool rocks of the cliff. After a few minutes Bill got up and headed for a faucet hidden behind one of the rocks. "Take some water," Bill instructed me. "It's important to have enough fluids when you run."

I bent down and drank from the faucet. Nothing had ever tasted so good!

"I didn't know I was that thirsty," I told Bill, taking a deep breath.

"How do you feel?" he asked.

"Great," I told him, "absolutely great."

I'd wanted to ask Bill for a long time about his past, and now seemed to be the perfect time. "Bill, forgive me for saying this," I began, "but when I first saw you, the last time I was in Newport—well, you were kind of on the plump side."

Bill threw back his head and laughed. "I sure was!" he exclaimed. "That was the summer I was supposed to be here for just a few months." Suddenly his laughter faded, and he slumped back against the rocks. He sat silently for a few moments. Finally he said, "That was before the accident. See, Penny, there was an accident in my life, too."

I still didn't say anything. Pulling off my right shoe, I shook some sand out of it. Rusty lay down beside us and promptly went to sleep. "They're nice shoes, Penny," Bill said, but his voice sounded sad now, slow and deliberate. "I'm glad you have good ones. It's important." Still I sat quietly because I knew he wasn't through with his story.

"My folks were going to be working hard that summer," he finally continued. "They were opening a factory for making electronic parts. They knew they were going to be too busy to come home on any kind of a schedule. So I came to visit my grandparents here in Newport for the summer."

"Where was your home?" I asked.

"Huntington Beach, in southern California," he answered. "My parents had a small business there, but gradually they were moving everything down to San Diego. They spent a lot of time searching for the right place. A salesman with a private plane set up a trip for them one day, and off they flew. Something happened over the mountains, and they crashed. That was my accident, Penny."

"My grandfather told me that you'd lost them both," I said quietly.

"So, anyhow," he went on, "that's how I stayed on. My uncle helped sell the house and the business, and my grandparents and I went back for just a couple of days for the funeral."

He took off both his shoes and shook out the sand. "I guess I was sick for a while—really sick. I couldn't eat. I would have lost weight anyhow, but the pounds rolled off when I started to run. It was right after the accident. We'd just come back, and I was walking down on the beach. What I really wanted to do was just walk right into those waves and let them swallow me up. Instead, I started running so fast I couldn't catch my breath, and I remember thinking that maybe if I ran fast enough, my heart would give out and I'd drop dead, and that would be that. I ran and ran, even though I didn't know how to breathe properly at that time. I ran so far I finally dropped with exhaustion. My heart was pounding like a drum inside my ears. I learned one thing that day. It's hard to run and feel sorry for yourself at the same time. My head started to clear, and I swear, Penny, it's the truth, I heard my dad telling me that I had my whole life ahead of me and to make sure I made something out of it. And as sure as I'm sitting here now, I could hear my mom telling me that if I wanted to run, I should learn all I could about it and do it the right way." I could tell from his voice that he was on the edge of tears and yet, on the edge of a laugh, too. "OK," he said abruptly. "We're wasting time. We've got to keep running. Come on, Rusty, this means you, too!"

Quickly we slipped on our running shoes, and in seconds Bill and I were jogging side by side, Rusty way ahead of us again.

I knew Bill a little better now. I liked him. I really liked him. And like sometimes turns into love. I think then, running beside him, that's exactly what happened.

Chapter Fifteen

Frankie stayed in the hospital one week, enjoying the lavish attention we all showered on him and adjusting to the fact that he would have to use crutches for some time. I had to admit I really missed the little guy after a day or so. In fact, I was crazy enough to tell him when he came home.

He gave me a bear hug, and his skinny arms around my neck felt good. "I missed you, too!" he confessed. I figured he would be OK as a brother when he finally grew up.

Many things happened in the next few weeks. The rooms were finished; the plumbing was completely replaced in the bathrooms; and great parts of the roof were patched. Bill and a hired painter started painting the outside of the house. My grandfather was busy refinishing the dining room table and its leaves and Mom discovered a lace tablecloth that had been packed away by my grandmother a long time ago. Grandad told us that she had crocheted it that large because she'd always thought they were going to have a big family, but only my mother had arrived. Now it would be put to use for the first time. The place was looking more and more like a boardinghouse.

We were all working hard, but Bill and I still managed to find time to be alone. We ran on the beach with Rusty each morning before breakfast. We spent every free moment we had together. Bill showed me places I'd never been, and some I had, but wanted to see again. Jessica was right. My summer was turning into the best ever.

One day we were sitting silently on the beach, watching the waves crash upon the sand. Bill stroked my hair lazily. All of a sudden he stood up and pulled a piece of paper out of his back pocket. "Sign," he commanded me.

"What?" I took the paper, puzzled.

"Just sign!" he repeated.

"Wait a minute."

"Here's a pen," he said, whipping one out of his shirt pocket and sitting down beside me again.

"What is it?" I asked as he shoved the pen into my hand.

"It's the Summer Cancer Run, ten kilometers," he answered. "It's kind of to wind up the summer. Most of the people who enter are just casual runners, and so it's not really competitive."

"Ten kilometers," I repeated.

"Yeah, like six point two miles. No big thing."

"Over six miles!" I turned to face him, the pen poised in midair. "What is this, Bill Davis? You want *me* to enter? Are you nuts? I can barely finish two miles without collapsing."

"Come on, Penny, just sign," he said.

"No way, Bill! Absolutely no way!"

He put his arm around my shoulders and squeezed me to him. "Penny, I'm signing up. It's going to take a big part of the day. You know, the festival goes with it all. I just thought you'd like to run with me."

"I'll stand on the sidelines and cheer for you," I told him, refolding the paper. "How long have you carried this thing in your pocket? It's falling apart."

"Most of the summer." He smiled sheepishly. "I was too scared to ask you. Look, the registration fee goes to cancer research; so it's a good cause. Now you just sign right here, and I'll drop this in the box at the pool."

"What's the registration fee?"

"Four dollars."

"OK," I told him. "I'll donate the four dollars. I'll give it to you when we get back to the house. But if you think I'm going to be dumb enough to enter that race, you're crazier than I thought!"

"Why won't you enter?"

"I can't win, silly," I told him simply.

"It isn't to win," he said, and his voice sounded angry and frustrated. "It would be farther than you've ever run, but if you did it, you'd be winning over the stubborn, dumb part of you that says you can't do it. See, you'd be beating that other girl, the one in you who makes things so hard for you. Now sign," he said again, placing the paper in my fingers.

He took me in his arms and kissed my earlobe. I struggled to free myself, but I felt all my resistance flowing away. I closed my eyes, and his kisses found my cheek and then my mouth. My hand relaxed, and I dropped the pen. He didn't seem to notice, but then when our kiss was over, he knew exactly where to bend over to scoop up the pen.

"Silly, I can't," I said. I stood up and walked away slowly down the beach.

Chapter Sixteen

The next morning my grandfather got to the phone before anyone else, catching it on the second ring. I thought it was one of the workmen calling or maybe Dr. Dunn, who was lining up tenants. He had already found an older married couple to do the cooking and minor repair work in return for board. My grandfather called me to the phone.

My mother and I went into the living room, and Grandad put the phone down. "That's Bill on the phone for you, Penny. Seems like his grandmother's sister is sick up in Portland. Bill's driving them there, and he'll be gone a week, maybe more."

I picked up the phone, and Bill and I talked briefly. After I hung up, I stood for a moment, thinking. I felt relieved, but miserable at the same time. I wanted to spend as much time with Bill as possible, but I knew I'd really disappointed him by not signing up for the race. So, I was miserable I wouldn't see him, but relieved that I wouldn't have to argue with him about the race.

"You didn't run this morning," my mother said on her way back to the kitchen to make breakfast.

"No, I was too tired. I stayed up too late last night."

She gave me a funny look but said nothing. I didn't feel like telling her what had happened the day before with Bill and that I had decided not to go running with him that morning.

Another call came just after we finished our breakfast. It was Giddy. "Hi," she started, somewhat breathlessly. "Got a favor to ask, Penny. Please don't say no because we're desperate here—"

"For a friend like you I'd do anything," I said, laughing. What can I do for you?"

"OK," she said. "There's no one here who can do this as well as you can. You know I have a class of kids, age eight through ten, and we're training them to compete with kids from other counties. Jan and I have been able to handle almost everything, crawl, backstroke, breaststroke, but we are both lousy at the butterfly. I mean *terrible*! We need someone to look at the kids and tell them what they're doing wrong."

"There's Ruth Bailey. She was pretty good a couple of years ago," I said. "Why don't you call her?"

"She lives in Washington now."

"Oh," I said helplessly. "And you want me to come and teach the butterfly?"

"Right!" Giddy said. "You don't even have to get in the pool! Just take a look at them. Oh, Penny, they want to be able to compete. Knowing the butterfly will make their performances complete!"

"OK," I told her, and I could hear her sigh with relief.

"They're going to love it!" she exclaimed. "Thanks a ton, Penny!"

Giddy said she'd pick me up the next morning at eight. I told my mother, and she smiled with approval. "Passing on information is fun," she said. "I remember how lucky you were to have Donna Mathew for your first coach."

Donna had been on an Olympic team, and she had spent a few years after that instructing our swimming team at Carousel Elementary. These kids would be just about the same age as I had been when I started out. It was important for them to learn good habits from the very start, and I smiled when I thought of being the person who would help them. At least I was good for something!

The next morning I put on my white shorts and blue T-shirt, then wound my hair up in a knot and secured it to the top of my head. It was important that the kids see my shoulders when I showed them the proper movements of the butterfly.

"Aren't you wearing your bathing suit?" my mother asked as I passed her in the upstairs hall.

"No, no need," I told her. "A coach often instructs from poolside."

"Hmmph!" my mother mumbled under her breath.

Giddy was driving her father's station wagon. "I hate it, but my car is in the shop again," she told me. "Seems it would rather be there than with me!"

"I'm getting my license in the fall," I told her. "I would have had it already if it hadn't been for the accident. But I won't have a car to drive anyway, because we have only one in our family."

"Maybe your dad will buy you one when he

makes a million from his first book!" Giddy said happily.

"Dreamer!" I laughed.

The pool swarmed with kids of all ages. Ron had three rows of little boys lined up over to one side. I could hear his deep voice booming out, cautioning the boys not to run in the slippery puddles around the pool.

Jan was sitting at the front desk, and she smiled at me when I entered with Giddy. "I knew you couldn't stay away from us too long!" she yelled at me.

Giddy led me over to her class, and she introduced me proudly: "This is Penny Snow from Carousel, Ohio. She won the state championship for the butterfly year before last!" The kids looked at me, and their eyes widened in awe. Old familiar feelings started rushing through me, a flow of pride. It made me feel great!

Giddy addressed her class. "Now the butterfly is a competitive stroke, much faster than the others we've taught you. And it's tiring! It's not too good over long distances, but it's terrific for short bursts of intensive swimming." Giddy turned to me. "They're all yours, Penny."

I drew in a deep breath. "OK, everyone sit

down around me so that you can see," I told them. "First, I'm going to tell you what *not* to do. Don't throw your arms too far forward on recovery. Don't try to reach. If you find you tend to sink, quicken your speed a little. Keep your hips high by pulling in your stomach muscles, and don't make your leg action stiff from the hips."

The kids watched carefully as I went through the motions of a good butterfly. I showed them how my arms worked together and explained the dolphin kick. "In our meets we used the double dolphin kick, a double kick to each arm cycle," I told them. "Here, I'll show you what I mean."

I ran through the rules of competitive swimming, and those little kids took in every word. When I thought they'd understood, I decided it was time for them to enter the pool. We went through starts and turns for about ten minutes until I was pleased that they all had the right idea. Then we got down to the actual motions of a correct butterfly.

One girl, about nine, seemed to be having a hard time with recovery. She tried with the rest of them, but then stopped and pulled herself out of the water. Grabbing a towel, she threw it around her shoulders and went over to the bleachers where she sat down, all hunched over, making herself look even smaller.

I looked back at the kids in the water. They were doing great. I walked back to the girl on the bench. "Are you tired already?"

"Yes," she said sadly. "There's something wrong with me. I can't seem to keep up with anyone, not even the smallest ones."

"What's your name?"

"Tawny Price."

"That's a pretty name," I told her. "Tell you what, Tawny. I'll give you my special attention. Jump in, and I'll try to find out what's slowing you down."

She shrugged her shoulders, and I thought I saw a tear in her eye, but she stood up, dropped the towel, and went over to the side of the pool. She slid into the water and began her butterfly strokes. I could tell right away what her problem was. I called her over to the side. "Tawny, you're breathing too early in the stroke. It interrupts the backward push of your hands."

Tawny obediently shoved off again. "Too early, again," I called out.

Giddy came over to my side of the pool.

"Would you like to get in with her? She seems to be having so much trouble."

"Do you have a spare suit?"

"You know we do," Giddy said, smiling. She led me to the back showers where the girls kept the official pool suits. In minutes I was out again, this time dressed for business! With excitement and apprehension, I plunged into the pool.

Standing right next to Tawny, it was easy to correct her problem. After that she was off, keeping up with the rest of the group. When the practice was finally over and the girls had started to leave the pool area, Giddy and I rested on the bleachers. Tawny slid up to me. "I want to be really good someday, Penny, like you are. Do you think I could do it? Do you think I could be so good I could win my own trophy someday?"

As clear as if I'd heard them yesterday, Donna's first words to our swimming class came back to me. Why not give them to this little girl? Those words had helped me so much when I'd started out.

"Tawny," I said, "pick out the stroke you want to master and make it as perfect as you can, the way I was showing you today. Don't train against the best swimmer in your group or against national or Olympic times."

"But I want to beat them."

"Of course you do. You should be aware of those times, and your goal is to beat them, but you have to learn to train against *yourself*. It's your improvement that really counts."

I hadn't thought about those words in years, and I realized just how true they were. I hadn't raced in so long, I'd forgotten that the real competition was with oneself. I remembered one time when I'd come in second at a swim meet. And I hadn't felt bad because I'd beaten my own fastest time. The other girl had been faster, but that hadn't mattered. Suddenly I thought of Bill and his words about the race.

Giddy and I changed clothes for the ride home. "I can't tell you what you did for us today, Penny," she said as we walked toward her father's station wagon. "These kids really have the basics of a good butterfly now. And what you said to Tawny about not paying attention to the other kids around her, to try to better her own times—that should help her later, too, when she's facing the hard training."

"Maybe she'll get as far as the Olympics

someday," I said as I crawled in the passenger's side.

"Wouldn't that be funny," Giddy said as she settled herself behind the wheel. "They'd hand her the medal, she'd be on camera, and to the whole world she'd say, 'I want to thank Penny Snow!' "

Giddy and I both cracked up then. The whole day had been perfect. I would have given anything for Bill to be there. He would have been so proud of me!

Chapter Seventeen

I hate those paper-covered, leather-topped tables they make you sit on while you wait for the doctor to examine you. I've been on so many, sitting there in a white paper robe, the strings just barely holding everything together. It seems like the nurse just plops you there, goes away, and forgets about you entirely.

Dr. Dunn's examining room was no different from the one back home: same narrow leather table; same tiny room with a chair in one corner; a few white cabinets with mysterious instruments and potions in them; and a tiny, white-curtained window that I knew overlooked the parking lot, except that it was so high up that I couldn't look through it.

A painting hung on the wall, purposely put at eye level for a person sitting on the table as I was. It was an ocean scene because ocean scenes are supposed to be calming. But it didn't soothe my rattled nerves.

The door swung open at last, and my mother slipped through first, followed by Dr. Dunn. I've always liked my grandfather's doctor. He's not stuffy at all, and he has a nice, easy smile. He was smiling broadly now, two X rays in his right hand. He motioned for my mother to sit in the only available chair, and he perched on an examining stool. He prodded and poked my leg a little, just a quick examination. He'd done a thorough check-up the week before.

"Well, Penny," he started, "I've talked with your Ohio doctor, and she filled me in on your accident. These X rays we took last week show that things have healed quite well. A bit of advice, though," Dr. Dunn added. The room was very still. Even the curtains had stopped blowing. "Your mother told me about your involvement in sports before the accident and then about your hesitation to get back into them. She also says you've been running lately. That's good. I think you know, Penny, you can never expect to excel in sports as you used to. But you can and *should* participate in physical exercise of some kind. Keep your body moving smoothly so that it can develop its own memory system and work well even when you aren't consciously thinking of it. Now whatever you've been doing these last two months has been excellent. Keep up the good work!"

I sat up very straight on the table. "There's a ten-kilometer race this coming Saturday," I said, and my mother turned quickly to look at me. "Would it be OK—do you think it would hurt me to run that distance?"

The doctor's eyes widened, and my mother coughed. "Ten kilometers," he said thoughtfully. "That's over six miles."

"I'm used to running a little over two each morning," I told him. "In the last few days I've made it up to three."

"Then run a little over three," he said, smiling.

"But then I guess it would be dumb to enter," I told him, my voice trailing off to a whisper.

Dr. Dunn sat back on his stool and leaned against the wall. "You'll have to decide that one for yourself, Penny."

The doctor said goodbye, and I began to pick up my clothes. My mother helped me slide the paper gown off, and slowly I pulled on my jeans and shirt. "Don't look so glum; all the news is good," she told me, smiling again.

Never to win again, I thought, my eyes fixed on the ocean scene on the wall. *Never to come in first or hear the crowd screaming and shouting all for me. Never to feel those slaps on the back and those cries of "You were wonderful!"* All that good news my mother mentioned was making me absolutely miserable.

I pushed unhappily through the office door and out onto the street. A boy jogged through the parking lot, and for a split second I thought it was Bill. He had his arms raised in running position, and he streaked by in an instant.

"I didn't know you were even thinking of entering the race," my mother said, unlocking the passenger side of the Buick.

I didn't answer her. I was too busy thinking about the doctor's words. "Run a little over three." *Maybe three and a half*, I thought as I settled myself in the car. *Maybe four or five . . .*

Instead of five o'clock, I slid out of the darkened house at four-forty-five the next morning, determined to run three and a half full miles instead of the three I'd been doing all week. I felt the sand hug my feet comfortably on the first stretch. It was still dark, but over in the east the sun was struggling to wake up, casting a rosy light in the sky.

It was good to be alone for a while. So much was going on in my grandfather's house, I had been happy to escape it. The house staff would be moving in the day after my family left for Ohio. A few days later the boarders would be making the house their permanent home.

My grandfather had turned a small room downstairs into an office because he wanted to manage things. My mother said it was good for him; so she didn't interfere. The most wonderful new plan he had dreamed up was for the attic. He planned to divide it into small rooms for boarders' guests, who might have traveled some distance and needed a place to stay. Also, my grandfather promised us that whenever we wanted to visit from Ohio, we could use the attic.

My grandfather had cornered me one day, his expression serious. "Penny, I want you to come back and spend some of your summers with me."

I promised that I would. And it probably

would be fun to live in the boardinghouse for a couple of months and watch how things worked out with the "chosen group" as Grandad called them.

Mr. and Mrs. Gregory, the retired couple who would do the cooking and maintenance, had one of the upstairs back bedrooms. A retired nurse, Julia Mattson, would give her services in return for room and board. In the room that my mother had slept in, there would be the twin brothers from Ocean View. Mr. and Mrs. Hardy would share Frankie's room, and my bedroom would be occupied by the feisty Gunther sisters, also from Ocean View. The extra downstairs bedroom had been turned into a game room, and it now contained a television set, a home computer, video games, and a pool table, plus bookcases jammed full of interesting books.

I reached Norton's cliff and collapsed, leaning against the cool rocks. Rusty ran over to the faucet and looked at me with pleading eyes.

"OK, Rusty, I'll turn it on for you. Just give me a minute to rest."

The water trickled over his head, and he shook violently. I remembered one day when he'd done the same thing to Bill and me. I missed Bill so much, it hurt me to think about him. Closing my eyes, I rested against the cliff, thinking of him, wondering what he was doing. Did he miss me, too?

Rusty barked a few times, nudged me, and playfully jumped around in the sand by my feet, trying to get me to run again. "OK, Rusty, you win," I said wearily. "Get ready, and we'll do some serious running this time." I felt more than heard someone behind me, and I quickly struggled to my feet. It was too early for anyone to be on the beach.

"Penny." Bill stood before me, the sea breeze whipping at his hair. He smiled at me. "We got home late last night. I came down to see if you were running."

He walked toward me, and I ran into his arms. I felt the warmth of his breath on my neck. "Penny, I missed you so."

"And I missed you!"

"It was a terrible week. I wanted to call you, but I thought you might still be mad at me for trying to push you into the race."

"It was terrible for me, too," I told him, kissing his cheek. "And I thought you might still be mad at me for copping out."

He held me again, very close, the early rays of the sun streaming across the beach.

"I'm glad to see you haven't stopped running, Penny."

"I have to run," I told him, looking up into his dark blue eyes. "I'm getting in shape for the race."

Chapter Eighteen

The starting point of the race was the Embarcadero, a fancy hotel in Newport. From there, we'd run 3.1 hilly miles to Yaquina River, then retrace the course back to the hotel. The weather was cool and sunny the morning of the race, just perfect for running.

"It's a tough course," Bill told me as we drove toward the bay. "If you pace yourself, not too fast at the beginning so that you won't use all your energy in the first few miles, you should be able to finish. Just do your best." Then he explained the different categories. Runners were sorted by age group with a man and a woman in each group receiving a gold medal for finishing first. I'd be competing with girls fifteen to nineteen. Of course, Bill told me not to think about it as a competition, and I tried to remember my words to little Tawny Price at the pool, but I was having a hard time seeing it that way. Bill said there'd be some serious runners but also a lot of people entering just for the fun of it.

We'd gotten an early start so that we could check in with the race officials and stretch out a bit. Mom, Frankie, and Grandad were going to drive to the starting point later. Rusty had to be kept home because of all the excitement. Knowing him, he'd run ahead of the crowd the whole time and win the race!

If you're not used to it, 6.2 miles is a long way, and people were standing around talking about how long it would take to run. All you could hear from most of them was that they weren't in top form at the moment. It was the usual runners' talk, Bill had told me earlier.

"You're going to hear about all kinds of problems and symptoms," he'd told me, laughing. "Some of them will let you think they haven't been able to put one foot in front of the other all month. It's a tradition—or a superstition. If they admit they're feeling great, then they'll run poorly. But as soon as that gun cracks in the air, you'll see a bunch of instant cures."

He'd cautioned me, too, about position. "If you're too far forward, the runners behind you may knock you down as they pass, or shake you up a bit. If you're too far back, you'll have to wind your way forward through the mass. Start a little toward the rear. You can always pass some of them later on." He'd been in so many races, I figured he knew what he was talking about; so I clustered around the runners toward the rear, while he went forward a bit.

I waved at my mother and Frankie. They'd brought along folding beach chairs and were setting them up.

"Go get 'em, Penny," Grandad called to me.

"Go for it!" screamed my little brother.

I was suddenly aware of a girl standing beside me. Is this your first race?" she asked timidly.

"Yes," I told her. "I've been running every day for two months, but only on the beach and only about two or three miles at a time."

"I'm from Utah," she said. "We're here visiting my aunt and uncle. My uncle had me registered before I even knew about the race." She was kind of on the plump side. Everything about her was very round, but her face was absolutely beautiful. *She should lose some weight*, I thought.

"I'm visiting, too," I told her. "I'm from Carousel, Ohio."

"You certainly have a good cheering section," she said, smiling. "See over there?" She pointed to the other side of the street. "That's Aunt Carole, Uncle Wayne, and my father. They're all into sports," she went on, shoving her long, sandy hair out of her eyes. She reached down into the back pocket of her green shorts and found a rubber band. Quickly she tied her hair back, and I could see more of her face. She had nice, clear skin and eyes like the green marbles in one of my brother's games. Why had she let herself get so heavy?

"I know I'm too fat to run well," she said, reading my mind.

"Oh, not really," I lied, and I felt terribly embarrassed.

"It's a gland problem," she said. She went on about her totally perfect father and how he used to be a football star at college and how his brother was one of the greatest basketball players in the Pacific Northwest and how they were standing on that corner, waiting for her to win in her category. "No way am I going to win. I told them I couldn't. At home I've run a little at our school track, but never in a real race."

"They'll understand," I said.

"You know what would be just terrible?" she continued. "If I came in last! I mean, I'd die! Really die!"

"Oh, it wouldn't be that bad. What's your name? Mine is Penny Snow."

"June Peek," she said, wiping off the front of her shorts.

Then the loudspeaker buzzed, and a hush fell over the crowd. An announcer came on and said that the race would start in another minute or two. He told us to check our shoes and read the official race rules; then he cautioned us about the importance of taking the water offered to us at water stations and wished us luck. I thought that was funny because we all couldn't be lucky. There would be only one winner in each category.

I whispered to myself, "Good luck." I turned to June Peek. "I wish you luck," I told her, and I surprised myself because I really meant it. She would need it, and it seemed to matter so much to her.

Suddenly the gun cracked in the air, and the people around me were moving. A little girl about eight smacked into me right from the start, and when I looked up, June was way in front of me. She was running pretty well, but I knew her pace was too fast for the beginning of the race. Maybe if I could catch up to her, I'd tell her.

It took only a few minutes. I really felt fine, almost as good as I'd felt years ago when our gym class ran around the school track between basketball practices. Our teacher had tried to get some of us interested in the track team, but all I wanted to do was swim.

"Hey, June," I called over to her. "Watch your beginning pace. You'll tire too early and won't be able to give that extra kick at the end."

"Got to move!" she said, her breath coming in quick spurts. "As soon as my family can't see me, I'll slow down."

And she did just that. As soon as we rounded the first corner, she let up a whole lot, and before I knew it, she was far behind me. I kept my pace steady, but after two and a half miles, I started to tire. It was because my body had been conditioned for about that distance, I reasoned. *OK*, I psyched myself, *the next few miles are fresh ones. You're just starting on them*. My breathing came more easily, and I settled in for the next stretch.

At one point June showed up right beside me. "Better take it easier," I said. "Remember what I told you."

She gave me a little smile. "Thanks," she said, breathing heavily. "But I can't afford to let down."

She flew by me. *Poor June*, I thought. No one had ever taken her aside and taught her about running. Would her parents really be that upset if she came in last? Wouldn't they just be happy that she'd given it her very best?

We reached the halfway mark, and the mass of runners started back. I was in the last third or so of the group with the tail-enders. My hip and leg felt a little stiff now. I looked over and saw June. She was crumpled up under a tree with a side stitch. Bill had told me about those. They almost always happen when you're running fast and not breathing deeply enough, but they'll disappear quickly if you run more slowly.

I stopped running and walked over to her. A bunch of stragglers caught up to me and passed by.

"It's a stitch," I told June. "Breathe deeply. Use your stomach muscles. Come on, June. Breathe deeper! No one has ever died because of one. Come on, you're not trying!"

She moaned and tried. Finally she lifted her head and looked at me. "I think it's helping," she said feebly. "But you're losing time."

"I'm not losing anything," I assured her. "Now just keep on breathing like that."

It took her several minutes to recover. By that time, though, even the smallest of kids and the oldest of runners had sailed by us.

"We'll never catch up," she said, moaning.

"Sure we will," I told her. "Just keep with me. I'll do the pacing."

Side by side we ran. Her rubber band had snapped off, and her long hair bounced behind. Now and then I cautioned her about breathing.

"I'll just die if I come in last," she said over and over.

We had completed three-quarters of the race, scooping up paper cups of water at every station. Some people on the sides laughed at our being the tail-enders. I saw June wince in pain at that.

Again my hip and leg stiffened up. I tried to relax, thinking soothing thoughts, like the ocean and the sunsets in Newport—and Bill. I thought mostly of Bill and what he had grown to mean to me.

The race was almost over. We could see the finish line ahead and the crowd of racers who'd already crossed it. I remembered Bill's instructions, and I started the final push. At least I wouldn't come in last. I gave it all I had and streaked right past June. I could hear her gasping as I passed, and I turned to look back.

She looked absolutely miserable. Her hair hung limply around her shoulders, and even though I was still running, I could see tears sparkling in her green eyes. It meant so darn much to her. It shouldn't have, but it did. She should have been happy to finish at all. I thought of myself in those next few seconds. I would finish, too. I'd never really thought I would.

Then the strangest thing happened. Instead of increasing my pace, I slowed down. As she passed me, I called out to her. "Give it all you got now, June. Do your finishing kick! Go for it!"

For an instant she raised her hand and waved to me. It was the kind of wave you give to another driver when they let you slip into a long string of cars in a traffic jam.

I could see the Embarcadero now on Newport's bay front. The crowd was cheering even as the stragglers approached the finish line. June was now in front of me by several yards, and there was absolutely no one behind me, not even a little kid. But I was holding up my head, and I was finishing, just like everyone else! I'd done the ten kilometers.

Someone handed me two paper towels, and I wiped my face and then my neck and the whole front of me. I was laughing and crying, and the sweat was just pouring off me.

Then Bill was standing in front of me. He broke through the crowds of cheering people and walked toward me. I felt a little dizzy, and without realizing it, I leaned against his chest and then just collapsed on him.

He squeezed me tightly, ran his fingers through my soaked hair, and brushed my hot cheeks with his kisses. That was when I noticed the ribbon around his neck. The gold medal hung proudly from the ribbon. I looked up to his face, and I said, "Oh, Bill, you're one of the winners! I'm so happy for you!"

He smiled and hugged me to him again. "And you came all the way, too," he said. "Penny, I'm so proud of you!"

"Oh, Bill, I did it, I finished," I cried. "I thought I'd never be able to!"

"Never say never." Bill smiled at me.

I looked around and found June getting a hug from her father and uncle and aunt. She was all tears and smiles at the same time. Her eyes caught mine, and I knew we had an understanding.

Bill let me go and began struggling with the ribbon. Pulling it up over his head, he slid the ribbon and medal over my soaked hair, arranging it tenderly on me.

"Why?" I asked, puzzled.

"It's yours," he said. "You won it." He wouldn't let me take it off. A couple of people stopped and asked me what I won, but Bill just told them that I'd reached a goal I'd set for myself, which made me a winner just like he was.

"Hey, Penny," I heard a call. It was Giddy. "Jan and I came down to watch the race. We didn't know you'd be running. Penny, I can't believe you ran six miles."

"Six point two," I reminded her. "And I feel great."

"You do, huh? Then how about coming by the pool tomorrow for a little swim? Anyone who can run that far has got to be in good enough shape for a few laps."

I smiled up at Bill. "Giddy, I used to think I could never swim again. But you know what? I think I'll give it a try."

We hope you enjoyed reading this book. All the titles currently available in the Sweet Dreams series are listed on the next two pages. They are all available at your local bookshop or newsagent, though should you find any difficulty in obtaining the books you would like, you can order direct from the publisher, at the address below. Also, if you would like to know more about the series, or would simply like to tell us what you think of the series, write to:

Kim Prior,
Sweet Dreams,
Transworld Publishers Limited,
Century House,
61–63 Uxbridge Road,
London W5 5SA.

or
Kiri Martin
c/o Corgi & Bantam Books New Zealand,
9 Waipareira Avenue,
Henderson,
Auckland,
New Zealand.

To order books, please list the title(s) you would like, and send together with your name and address, and a cheque or postal order made payable to TRANSWORLD PUBLISHERS LIMITED. Please allow cost of book(s) plus 20p for the first book and 10p for each additional book for postage and packing.

20323 1	**P.S. I LOVE YOU (1)**	*Barbara Conklin*	£1.25
20325 8	**THE POPULARITY PLAN (2)**	*Rosemary Vernon*	£1.25
20327 4	**LAURIE'S SONG (3)**	*Suzanne Rand*	£1.25
20328 2	**PRINCESS AMY (4)**	*Melinda Pollowitz*	£1.10
20326 6	**LITTLE SISTER (5)**	*Yvonne Greene*	£1.10
20324 X	**CALIFORNIA GIRL (6)**	*Janet Quin-Harkin*	£1.25
20604 4	**GREEN EYES (7)**	*Suzanne Rand*	£1.25
20601 X	**THE THOROUGHBRED (8)**	*Joanna Campbell*	65p
20744 X	**COVER GIRL (9)**	*Yvonne Greene*	£1.25
20745 8	**LOVE MATCH (10)**	*Janet Quin-Harkin*	£1.25
20787 3	**THE PROBLEM WITH LOVE (11)**	*Rosemary Vernon*	£1.25
20788 1	**NIGHT OF THE PROM (12)**	*Debra Spector*	£1.25
17779 6	**THE SUMMER JENNY FELL IN LOVE (13)**	*Barbara Conklin*	£1.10
17780 X	**DANCE OF LOVE (14)**	*Jocelyn Saal*	£1.10
17781 8	**THINKING OF YOU (15)**	*Jeanette Nobile*	£1.10
17782 6	**HOW DO YOU SAY GOODBYE? (16)**	*Margaret Burman*	75p
17783 4	**ASK ANNIE (17)**	*Suzanne Rand*	£1.25
17784 2	**TEN BOY SUMMER (18)**	*Janet Quin-Harkin*	75p
17791 5	**LOVE SONG (19)**	*Anne Park*	75p
17792 3	**THE POPULARITY SUMMER (20)**	*Rosemary Vernon*	£1.25
17793 1	**ALL'S FAIR IN LOVE (21)**	*Jeanne Andrews*	£1.10
17794 X	**SECRET IDENTITY (22)**	*Joanna Campbell*	£1.25
17797 4	**FALLING IN LOVE AGAIN (23)**	*Barbara Conklin*	£1.25
17800 8	**THE TROUBLE WITH CHARLIE (24)**	*Jay Ellen*	£1.25
17795 8	**HER SECRET SELF (25)**	*Rhondi Vilott*	£1.10
17796 6	**IT MUST BE MAGIC (26)**	*Marian Woodruff*	£1.10
17798 2	**TOO YOUNG FOR LOVE (27)**	*Gailanne Maravel*	£1.10
17801 6	**TRUSTING HEARTS (28)**	*Jocelyn Saal*	£1.25
17813 X	**NEVER LOVE A COWBOY (29)**	*Jesse Dukore*	95p
17814 8	**LITTLE WHITE LIES (30)**	*Lois I. Fisher*	£1.25
17839 3	**TOO CLOSE FOR COMFORT (31)**	*Debra Spector*	95p
17840 7	**DAYDREAMER (32)**	*Janet Quin-Harkin*	95p
17841 5	**DEAR AMANDA (33)**	*Rosemary Vernon*	£1.25
17842 3	**COUNTRY GIRL (34)**	*Melinda Pollowitz*	95p
17843 1	**FORBIDDEN LOVE (35)**	*Marian Woodruff*	95p
17844 X	**SUMMER DREAMS (36)**	*Barbara Conklin*	£1.25
17846 6	**PORTRAIT OF LOVE (37)**	*Jeanette Nobile*	95p
17847 4	**RUNNING MATES (38)**	*Jocelyn Saal*	£1.25
17848 2	**FIRST LOVE (39)**	*Debra Spector*	£1.25
17849 0	**SECRETS (40)**	*Anna Aaron*	85p

17850 4	**THE TRUTH ABOUT ME AND BOBBY V (41)**	*Janetta Johns*	£1.10
17851 2	**THE PERFECT MATCH (42)**	*Marian Woodruff*	£1.10
17850 2	**TENDER LOVING CARE (43)**	*Anne Park*	95p
17853 9	**LONG DISTANCE LOVE (44)**	*Jesse Dukore*	95p
17069 4	**DREAM PROM (45)**	*Margaret Burman*	£1.10
17070 8	**ON THIN ICE (46)**	*Jocelyn Saal*	85p
17071 6	**TE AMO MEANS I LOVE YOU (47)**	*Deborah Kent*	£1.25
17072 4	**DIAL L FOR LOVE (48)**	*Marian Woodruff*	£1.25
17073 2	**TOO MUCH TO LOSE (49)**	*Suzanne Rand*	£1.25
17074 0	**LIGHTS, CAMERA, LOVE (50)**	*Gailanne Maravel*	£1.25
17075 9	**MAGIC MOMENTS (51)**	*Debra Spector*	£1.25
17076 7	**LOVE NOTES (52)**	*Joanna Campbell*	£1.25
17087 2	**GHOST OF A CHANCE (53)**	*Janet Quin-Harkin*	£1.25
17088 0	**I CAN'T FORGET YOU (54)**	*Lois I. Fisher*	£1.25
17089 9	**SPOTLIGHT ON LOVE (55)**	*Nancy Pines*	95p
17090 2	**CAMPFIRE NIGHTS (56)**	*Dale Novack*	95p
17871 7	**ON HER OWN (57)**	*Suzanne Rand*	95p
17872 5	**RHYTHM OF LOVE (58)**	*Stephanie Foster*	95p
17873 3	**PLEASE SAY YES (59)**	*Alice Owen Crawford*	95p
17874 1	**SUMMER BREEZES (60)**	*Susan Blake*	95p
17875 X	**EXCHANGE OF HEARTS (61)**	*Janet Quin-Harkin*	95p
17876 8	**JUST LIKE THE MOVIES (62)**	*Suzanne Rand*	95p
24150 8	**KISS ME, CREEP (63)**	*Marian Woodruff*	£1.10
24151 6	**LOVE IN THE FAST LANE (64)**	*Rosemary Vernon*	£1.10
24152 4	**THE TWO OF US (65)**	*Janet Quin-Harkin*	£1.25
24153 2	**LOVE TIMES TWO (66)**	*Stephanie Foster*	£1.25
24180 X	**I BELIEVE IN YOU (67)**	*Barbara Conklin*	95p
24181 8	**LOVEBIRDS (68)**	*Janet Quin-Harkin*	95p
24254 7	**CALL ME BEAUTIFUL (69)**	*Shannon Blair*	95p
24255 5	**SPECIAL SOMEONE (70)**	*Terri Fields*	95p
24355 1	**TOO MANY BOYS (71)**	*Celia Dickenson*	95p
24356 X	**GOODBYE FOREVER (72)**	*Barbara Conklin*	95p
24357 8	**LANGUAGE OF LOVE (73)**	*Rosemary Vernon*	95p
24381 0	**DON'T FORGET ME (74)**	*Diana Gregory*	95p
24382 9	**FIRST SUMMER LOVE (75)**	*Stephanie Foster*	95p
24385 3	**THREE CHEERS FOR LOVE (76)**	*Suzanne Rand*	95p
24387 X	**TEN-SPEED SUMMER (77)**	*Deborah Kent*	95p
24384 5	**NEVER SAY NO (78)**	*Jean F. Capron*	95p
24971 1	**STAR STRUCK (79)**	*Shannon Blair*	£1.10
24386 1	**A SHOT AT LOVE (80)**	*Jill Jarnow*	£1.10
24688 7	**SECRET ADMIRER (81)**	*Debra Spector*	£1.10
24383 7	**HEY, GOOD LOOKING! (82)**	*Jane Polcovar*	£1.10
24823 5	**LOVE BY THE BOOK (83)**	*Anne Park*	£1.10
24718 2	**THE LAST WORD (84)**	*Susan Blake*	£1.10
24890 1	**THE BOY SHE LEFT BEHIND (85)**	*Suzanne Rand*	£1.25
24945 2	**QUESTIONS OF LOVE (86)**	*Rosemary Vernon*	£1.10
24891 X	**WRONG KIND OF BOY (88)**	*Shannon Blair*	£1.25

Dear SWEET DREAMS reader,

Since we started publishing SWEET DREAMS almost two years ago, we have received hundreds of letters telling us how much you like the series and asking for details about the books and the authors.

We are getting to know quite a lot about our readers by now and we think that many of you would like a club of your own. That's why we're setting up THE SWEET DREAMS CLUB.

If you would like to become a member, just fill in the details below and send it to me together with a cheque or postal order for £1.50 (payable to The Sweet Dreams Club) to cover the cost of our postage and administration. Your membership package will contain a special SWEET DREAMS membership card, and a SWEET DREAMER newsletter packed full of information about the books and authors, beauty tips, a fascinating quiz and lots more besides (including a fabulous special offer!).

Now fill in the coupon (in block capitals please), and send, with payment, to:

The Sweet Dreams Club,
Freepost (PAM 2876),
London W5 5BR.

N.B. No stamp required.

I would like to join The Sweet Dreams Club.

Name:..

Address:..

....

I enclose a cheque/postal order for £1.50, made payable to The Sweet Dreams Club.